RIDE DOWN THE WIND

WAYNE BARTON

"Don't come back, Jess Faver," Nantahe said. *"I'm just another Apache now, and you're just another white-eye. If I see you again, I kill you."*

Once they had been like brothers —Army scout Jess Faver and his Apache friend Nantahe. When the army decided to imprison its own Indian scouts and transport them to a military reservation in Florida, it wasn't hard for Jess to slip Nantahe a key to help him break away from the transport train. But when Nantahe and his companions made their escape, they killed one of the soldiers who had been guarding them, despite Nantahe's promise to Faver of no bloodshed. Now it was up to Jess to bring back Nantahe,

(continued on back flap)

RIDE DOWN THE WIND

RIDE DOWN THE WIND

WAYNE BARTON

DOUBLEDAY & COMPANY, INC.
GARDEN CITY, NEW YORK
1981

All of the characters in this book are fictitious, and any resemblance to actual persons, living or dead, is purely coincidental.

28218

ISBN: 0-385-17525-6
Library of Congress Catalog Card Number 80-2950
Copyright © 1981 by Wayne Barton
All Rights Reserved
Printed in the United States of America
First Edition

For
J. Sam Barton
(1903-1976)

RIDE DOWN THE WIND

CHAPTER 1

The sentry was a Negro, one of the buffalo soldiers of the 10th Cavalry. He was a young man, not long in service, and he had been careless. Now he lay face down beside the railway embankment, a few yards from the nearest car of the train. A steady rain churned the ground to mud around him. Rain fell sullenly on his blue cavalry greatcoat, washing the dark stain of blood from the heavy wool. In the soft light of the lanterns, he almost might have been sleeping, but Jess Faver knew he was dead.

Faver stared down at the body, hardly aware of the silent troopers around him or of the presence of old Ben Wade, the detail's other interpreter, at his shoulder. He felt a sick certainty that this was his fault, his responsibility. He'd had Nantahe's word there would be no killing, but something had gone terribly wrong.

"They took his pistol and carbine," Ben Wade rasped. A couple of the troopers looked at him, but no one answered. "Ever-how many Apaches got out, they'll have at least two guns."

"At least," Faver said. He looked rather like an Indian himself, with rain-slick black hair plastered above a lean, windburned face. His impassive blue eyes gave no hint of the sickness that twisted at his guts.

Like Wade and the others on the train, Faver had been awakened by shouts and the crack of a carbine. Unlike them, he'd been sure he knew what was happening. He'd been expecting it since the threat of flash floods had forced the prison train onto this lonely siding just before dark. An unscheduled stop and a rainy night would be all the edge Nantahe would need to escape, quick and clean and with nobody hurt. Faver had believed that until he saw the body on the ground.

"'Ten-shun," someone snapped. The cavalrymen stiffened as

Major Randall strode into the circle of light. The major made an impatient gesture.

"Rest. How did this happen? Who gave the alarm?"

There was a moment's hesitation. Then one of the privates stepped forward, his hands twisting nervously on the stock of his carbine.

"I—I did, sir. It was my time to pull guard, and I come to find Davy—Private Greer, sir." He glanced involuntarily at the body. "He was here. I fired in the air and hollered for the sergeant of the guard. But I didn't see nothing."

"None of the other posts reported anything, sir," a tall sergeant added. "I set a squad to checking the train. Chan-desi and Nan-tahe and Chicuelo are missing. They were chained together up in the first coach with the wild ones, and they got the lock open some way."

"I see. Well done, Sergeant."

Randall was silent for a moment. He was a short man, his stockiness emphasized by his rumpled uniform. He might not look like much of a soldier, if a man failed to notice the tight-lipped mouth or the cold gray eyes beneath his bushy brows. The eyes moved to Faver, held him.

"You wouldn't know how Nantahe opened his shackles?"

"No," Faver lied.

"I see." Randall glanced at the listening troopers and left it at that. Heedless of the mud, he knelt beside the dead trooper.

Faver looked away. The train was dark and silent, but he knew its passengers were watching. There were almost two hundred Apaches on board—sixty Army scouts and their families. At least, the men had been scouts last week. Now they were government prisoners, headed for a military reservation in Florida.

The trail that led them there had had its beginnings months ago, during the final campaign against Geronimo. The Army scouts, white and Apache, had carried the fighting right to Geronimo's door. They'd tracked him into Mexico, cornered him, finally arranged for the surrender of his band. By all rights, they should have been heroes, but General Crook, who'd recruited the scouts, had been replaced as commander of the Department of Arizona by Nelson Miles. Miles didn't trust Indians, not even those who drew Army pay. He disbanded the scout companies and sent the men back to their reservations. At the same time, he proposed a plan to end the Apache troubles for good.

Geronimo and his followers were herded onto a train and sent to Fort Marion, Florida, so that they could never threaten Arizona again. Then Miles ordered a roundup of others he considered troublemakers. Sixty Chiricahua scouts were arrested without warning. A train was readied to carry them to the same prison as the hostiles they'd helped capture. One of the scouts was Nantahe.

Faver had seen Nantahe in the old guardhouse at Camp Bowie. Against orders, a friendly sentry slipped him inside. Most of the Apaches turned their backs on him, but a few—Chicuelo had been one, he remembered—stared at him with open hatred.

"A bad time, Jess," Nantahe said. He rose from a bunk along the wall, slowly, like an old man. He had resisted arrest. His face was bruised and swollen, and leg irons clinked on his ankles.

"It is a bad thing they do," he said. "We have done nothing wrong."

"I know. Look, I'll be on the train. Randall wants me to interpret." He spread his hands helplessly. "I talked to Randall, even went to the colonel. They don't have any choice. The orders come straight from Washington."

Nantahe said nothing. Faver couldn't meet his eyes.

"I can't help it, Nantahe. There's nothing I can do."

For a moment, Nantahe's shoulders slumped and something like desperation showed in his face.

"*Sikisn—*?"

Then his chin came up. His expression hardened, and his words were cold and proud: "We have done no wrong." He was an Apache. He would not beg, not even from his white brother, not even for his freedom.

And why should he? Faver thought in sudden anger. Should Nantahe, who'd saved Faver's life a dozen times, have to beg for a brother's due? If it were Jess being taken to prison, Nantahe wouldn't stop to sort out right and wrong, wouldn't submit to the orders of uniformed fools.

It wasn't hard for Faver to get hold of the key, nor to slip it to Nantahe at the depot.

"If you get loose, head for the old *ranchería* on the Río Conchos. I'll meet you there when I can."

Nantahe nodded, and Faver looked closely at him. He didn't know afterward just why he'd done it, but he reached out and caught Nantahe's wrist.

"It's a long run to Mexico, Nantahe, but you'll be able to live there. This'll all blow over in a few months, as long as there's no blood spilled. Promise me you'll stay out of trouble."

"I promise, *sikisn*." Nantahe's eyes were hooded. "No blood."

Faver shook his head. He'd had Nantahe's word, but it hadn't been enough. There were three Apaches out in the night somewhere, and one of them had managed to smuggle a knife aboard the train. Faver didn't know which one it had been, but he meant to find out.

"He's been dead about an hour, looks like. The hostiles will have a good start." Randall studied Faver for a moment, then abruptly rose to his feet. "There's nothing more we can do until daylight. Sergeant, dismiss the men. Double the sentries, and have the others get some sleep." His voice softened. "And take Private Greer to the baggage coach, out of the rain."

He turned away, then glanced back.

"Mr. Wade, Mr. Faver, report to me in the telegraph office in ten minutes."

The sergeant issued orders. Some of the men moved off to take over the sentry posts, and the rest drifted back toward the troop coach. Two cavalrymen lifted the dead man and carried him toward the train, the sergeant leading the way with a lantern.

"You gonna stay out in the wet, young feller?" Ben Wade asked. He clapped a hand on Faver's shoulder and gestured toward the coach. "If the major don't want us right away, I reckon I could find a drink to warm us up."

Faver shook his head. "I guess not, Ben. You go ahead. I'll see you in the office."

"Hmmph." Wade spat in the mud. "Suit yourself."

He limped off toward the cars, and Faver felt a moment's regret. Wade had been one of General Crook's civilian packers until a leg wound had ended his active campaigning. He was an old hand, and was said to be a good one, and there was no point in making him mad. Still, Faver didn't want company just now.

He stood alone in the rain until the doors of the baggage car closed on the troopers and their burden. When he turned away, his face was set. He knew what he wanted to do; now it was just a matter of convincing Randall. Faver thought about that and almost smiled. Convincing Randall might be a problem.

The telegraph office was a single, barnlike room, divided down the middle by a roughly built wooden counter. Major Randall stood impatiently on one side of the counter. The night operator sat on the other side, glaring with sleepy resentment at three telegraph blanks covered with Randall's tiny printing. Neither glanced up as Faver came in and leaned against the counter.

"There won't be anybody much awake up the line tonight," the operator was saying. "It would be better to wait—"

"Now," Randall cut in firmly. "Get this out to the commandant at Fort Concho at once. And wait for the answer."

The operator shrugged with theatrical resignation and turned to his key. Hiding a curse under cover of a yawn, he began tapping out a call. Randall watched for a moment, then turned his attention to Faver.

"Good. Where's Mr. Wade?"

"He'll be along, Major." Faver pulled off his dripping slicker and dropped it on a chair. "Reckon we'll be able to follow the Apaches?"

Randall glared at him. "I won't, and you know it. I have a train to move."

"Yeah. I know."

The major reddened at Faver's tone. "That's right, mister. I obey orders, even the ones I don't like. But you don't understand—"

He broke off abruptly as the door swung open again. Ben Wade came in, bringing with him a strong odor of whiskey. He sank into a chair and wiped his face.

"Still coming down out there. Probably it'll pass on by morning, though."

"Probably." Randall's voice was calm again. "I've telegraphed for patrols along the border, and to warn county sheriffs between here and Mexico to watch for the fugitives. And I've asked for a patrol from Fort Davis to follow their trail in the morning."

"They won't leave much trail, Major." Wade fished in his pocket for a plug of tobacco, rolled it in his hands. "And the patrol better look out. That Chicuelo is a bad one. I remember him from the old days, with Cochise."

"That doesn't mean much. A lot of the scouts were hostiles before Crook took them on."

Faver's protest was automatic, but actually he wasn't so sure. Chicuelo was in his middle forties, a lean man with a tight, thin-lipped mouth. He was a tough and effective scout, but he had changed sides before—and someone had murdered the sentry.

"I'm surprised at Chan-desi," Randall said. "The old man must be pushing seventy. I didn't think he'd try to escape."

"He's Nantahe's mother's brother," Faver explained. "I expect he went along to look after Nantahe."

Wade gnawed off a chunk of the plug and settled it in his cheek. "Bad luck, all the same. They're three smart ones, and these Texas soldier-boys haven't had Apache troubles for years. That patrol'll be doing good to catch a smell of them."

"A good scout would help," Faver said. He looked at Randall, his face suddenly serious. "That patrol. I'd like to ride with it."

Randall snorted. "Would you? Which side would you be on?"

Faver straightened, meeting the major's gaze squarely. He hadn't wanted it this way, but the bitterness welled up in him and he couldn't fight it back.

"You want to prove what you're hinting, Major? Then you can get me sent to Florida, too. Might as well have us all on the reservation."

"You got one of my men killed, mister." Randall's voice was very soft. "If I could prove it, I'd see you hang."

Faver stared at him. He'd ridden scout for Randall for five rough years, he and Nantahe. He'd considered the stocky major a friend, but it looked like that was ending, too.

"You don't need me to translate," Faver said after a moment. "Ben can handle that, and the patrol will need a scout." He paused, then added, "And I know Nantahe."

Randall looked at him for a minute. The major's anger seemed to drain away. He looked tired, and older than Faver had ever seen him.

"Yes," he said slowly. "I suppose you do."

He rubbed a hand across his face, then nodded to Faver. There was no weariness in his eyes.

"I want them accounted for, mister. All three of them. Bring them back or kill them. Do you understand?"

Ben Wade had been watching with open-mouthed astonishment. He didn't seem to understand, but Faver heard the unspoken part clearly enough. *Or don't come back.*

"Reckon I do, Major. Anything else?"

"That's all. Be ready to ride at dawn."

Randall turned away, and Faver pushed through the door into the rainy night. He would be ready. He didn't have many belongings to worry about, just his saddle and blanket roll and a troop horse from the last car. He'd be traveling light, if you didn't count the memory of a murdered trooper and a promise that had died with him.

"Boy, what the hell?" Ben Wade had followed him out. He caught at Faver's arm. "What's going on? The way old Randall talked, you'd think that 'Pache was your brother."

"Yeah?" Faver thought about it. "Yeah, I guess you would."

But it wasn't really true, he thought. Nantahe wasn't only a brother. Since the night they'd first met, almost nine years ago, he'd been the only family Faver had.

CHAPTER 2

Andrew Jackson Faver had brought his family a long way from eastern Tennessee in the years after the Civil War. Jess had been too young to remember the war or the old home place near Greeneville. Andrew Faver had gone against his kin to fight in the Union Army, and he took his wife and son West the year the war ended.

Jess did remember the succession of settlements in Missouri and Kansas, and finally in New Mexico. He remembered the homestead that failed near Wagon Mound, the mining camps of White Oaks and Silver City. He'd grown up rootless, with a tight-knit family loyalty and a stubborn hill-country pride instilled by his parents, but with no real home until, when Jess was almost fourteen, the Favers came to Arizona.

"There's good land near Tucson, Molly," his father had said. "And we have a stake to start on now."

"Arizona?"

Molly Faver turned from the stove, seeming to consider. Jess, hunched over a spelling book at the table, kept his head down to hide a grin. His mother would protest now, he knew, just like always.

"Arizona," she repeated. "There are Apaches there."

"There are Apaches here," Andrew Faver pointed out. "Things have been quiet since that new general, Crook, took over." He stepped quickly forward and took her hands. "Molly, it's a chance to have something—something of our own. It may be our last chance. And the boy needs a place—"

"The boy needs a place to grow up," she finished, smiling. Her eyes went to Jess. "You quit eavesdropping and finish your lesson, young man. We have to pack. We're moving to our new home."

And the homestead the Favers proved up in the Tanque Verde

country was home. Andrew Faver farmed a little, ran a few head of stock, sold hay to the Army. For Jess, there was school in Tucson, chores around the place, and sometimes odd jobs around Tucson or old Fort Lowell. The rest of the time, there was all the mountain and desert country at his call.

Jess hunted the hills with a broken-down white nag and a single-shot Sharps, or wandered for hours at a time through the streets of Tucson, listening to stories of soldiers and cowmen, Mexican dandies, down-on-their-luck prospectors, and all the others who passed through the dusty town on the Santa Cruz. As far as he was concerned, the homestead was paradise.

Even when the Apache troubles started up again, the Favers seemed to be immune. Andrew Faver had bluntly refused to join in the hatred many of the old settlers felt toward all Apaches. "I don't hold with judging a man without a chance," he'd said. "And an Indian's a man."

If his neighbors disapproved, the soldiers from Fort Lowell and the Apaches themselves did not. Often, Jess sat in awe while old chief Eskimizin or another of the Apache leaders visited and smoked with his father. Other settlers lost stock, had horses run off or killed in their stalls, but none of it touched the Faver place. Andrew Faver even allowed Jess to continue his hunting trips. The Apaches knew the boy. They knew the Favers as friends.

The mistake Andrew Faver made, the mistake that cost him his life, was his assumption that all Apaches were the same. The band that came to his place in June of 1878 were from the north, along the Salt River. There were ten of them, eight young warriors and two women, riding south to join a new leader named Geronimo. All they knew about Faver was that he was white.

Jess had been in the hills that day. When he rode in at dusk, the low, spreading column of smoke still hung over the ruins of the cabin. He knew what had happened, and he saw the trail, dim enough but plain to him, stretching toward the south—but first there were things to do.

Dry-eyed in the cool night, Jess Faver scratched out a grave for his father and mother in one corner of the garden. Dry-eyed, he searched the shell of the cabin for supplies the raiders might have missed. The water of the rock *tinaja* was slimy with the blood and offal of a slaughtered steer, but Jess still had half a canteen, and he had his rifle.

Dry-eyed, he swung aboard his horse and followed the Apache trail. A sliver of moon gave him enough light, and there was a cold determination in his heart. He was sixteen years old.

Jess hadn't decided what he would do when he found the renegades, and he never got a chance to find out. He had dismounted to lead his horse across a stretch of broken rock when he heard a sudden movement behind him. He swung around, dropping the reins and bringing up the rifle. In the same instant, a man hurtled from the brush to his left, coming low and hard. Too late, Jess realized he'd been tricked.

The attacker's shoulder caught him in the chest, driving him backward. The white horse reared and shied away. Jess chopped downward with the rifle. The steel-shod butt thunked solidly into muscle, but the force of the man's headlong rush drove Jess backward to the ground.

The other man piled on top of him, hands grappling for the rifle. Jess immediately released it and smashed a fist into his opponent's face. The man grunted and relaxed his hold, and Jess squirmed free, clawing for his hunting knife.

Apaches! he thought. They wouldn't get him. If he could—

There were others there, wrestling him to the ground. He managed to kick somebody, but then he was pinned helplessly with a heavy hand clamped over his mouth. He gave up struggling and the first attacker bent over him.

Jess looked up into the eyes of a boy little more than a year older than he, a boy with the bound black hair and square-cut features of an Apache. His lip was split, and blood trickled slowly down his chin. Two older warriors held Jess, one kneeling on each arm. The boy leaned close, looking at him thoughtfully in the starlight. He raised a hand to dab at the blood on his face and smiled.

Jess threw his head backward, got his teeth into the hand across his mouth. The Apache on his right yelped and jerked away.

"You dirty murderers," Jess yelled. "You might kill me, but—"

The man he'd bitten hit him, a vicious backhand blow that sent colored lights dancing behind his eyes. He shook his head and sucked in a deep breath, but before he could launch into another shout, the young Apache spoke.

"Quiet!" His voice was barely louder than a whisper, but it carried such assurance, such urgency, that Jess hesitated. "Bad Apaches hear you. We're scouts. Nobody will hurt you."

"What—?"

Jess unconsciously lowered his voice. His question died in a dry throat, and he began suddenly to tremble. He hadn't thought to be afraid a moment before, but now, mixed with the sudden relief, he felt an almost paralyzing fear.

"You, Deltche." The young Indian spoke to the man with the bitten hand. "Go get the lieutenant. And watch who you hit. Next one, I may let him hit back."

The warrior came swiftly to his feet. Even in the near-darkness, Jess could see that he was several years older, and that his face was set in anger.

"Who you think you are, Nantahe? You don't talk to me like that."

The Apache called Nantahe rose catlike, his hand dropping smoothly to the haft of his knife. The third man, still kneeling beside Jess, tensed expectantly.

"I think I'm sergeant commanding this patrol, and I talk to you any way I like. Now, go get the lieutenant, unless you think you can slap me, too."

Deltche stood motionless, eyes locked with Nantahe's, as seconds stretched into a minute. Then the scout beside Jess relaxed, and Jess realized that some decision had been reached. A moment later, Deltche turned and stalked into the night.

Jess sat up, watching as Nantahe caught the reins of the white horse and tied the animal. The scout picked up the Sharps rifle and turned it in his hands, then knelt and offered it to Jess.

"You all right?"

Jess nodded. The trembling was gone, and he was holding tightly onto himself again, blocking out the things he knew he must not remember for a while.

"Wait," Nantahe murmured.

He squatted on his heels, the other scout beside him. Once, he touched the drying blood on his chin and smiled again, but said nothing more. At last, Jess heard the muffled sounds of movement, the clink of shod hooves on stone. Horsemen bulked out of the darkness, led by Deltche—cavalry, a half-troop patrol. The leading rider pulled up short, dismounted.

"Rest the men, Sergeant. Unbit for grazing. No fires, no smoking. We'll move in half an hour."

The order went down the line in a whisper, and the man who had spoken came across to Jess and the two Apaches.

"I'm Lieutenant Callahan, 3rd Cavalry." He looked at Nantahe, then back at Jess. "I understand you've been abusing my scouts."

"I thought they were Apaches."

Nantahe chuckled softly and Jess was suddenly confused.

"No, I mean—"

"I know what you mean, boy. But this is dangerous country. What brings you out here?"

Jess took a deep breath.

"A bunch of Ap—of hostiles hit our place this morning, down by Tanque Verde. I've been tracking them since sundown."

"You've been—" Callahan stopped as if he couldn't quite decide how to finish. He took off his hat and ran a hand through his hair. He was not a young man, and the harsh shadows made him look older still. "Son, just what did you propose to do when you caught them?"

Jess didn't answer, but his hands tightened on the stock of the Sharps until the knuckles were ivory-white. After a moment, Callahan shrugged.

"No matter. Your pa shouldn't have let you come out alone."

"He's dead."

"Sorry." Callahan didn't understand. "But your mother, then. Why—?"

Jess made a strangled sound. He couldn't keep it back now.

"Both of them. The hostiles. Today. They killed them both."

"Good God," Callahan whispered. Even the scouts stirred. Nantahe straightened and peered closely at Jess. There was an endless silence. Then Callahan shook his head.

"We'll get them, son, I swear. But I'll have to detail a man to take you back."

"Like hell you will!"

The words wrenched out through clenched teeth, punctuated by the snap of the rifle's hammer coming to full cock. Before the lieutenant or the scouts could move, the muzzle was centered on Callahan's chest. Slowly, Jess came to his feet.

"I know where they're going, and I aim to get there. Don't try to stop me."

Jess started to back away, paused.

"I have to," he said. "They were my kin."

He reached back to pull the bridle of his horse free. Callahan sat frozen, and the other soldiers didn't realize what was happening. Only Nantahe moved.

"Wait," he said urgently. He stood up, and the rifle swung to cover him. "You know where they're going?"

"I think so."

The Apache took a step forward, hands extended. "Show us, then. You can't go alone." He looked at Callahan. "He can ride with the scouts, Nan-tan. We can use him."

Callahan hesitated, then nodded. Jess lowered the Sharps a trifle, jerked it back up as Nantahe turned back to him.

"It's all right," the scout said gently. "My word. You put the gun down."

Jess looked deep into the Apache youth's eyes, then eased the rifle's hammer down. He hung his head for a moment and his shoulders shook. Nantahe touched his arm.

"You come. The scouts start now, ride ahead."

Jess swung into the saddle, unwilling to trust his voice to answer. Deltche led up three horses and the scouts mounted.

"Good," Nantahe said. "You show us. We'll get them now."

Jess never forgot that ride. He had seen cavalry patrols before, but never one that moved by night, without pack mules or remounts. The troopers carried their supplies in saddlebags, or slung across their backs. The pace never went above a walk, but it never slackened and the scouts had to push hard to stay ahead of the column.

"We chase the cut-offs, the bad ones," Nantahe said. "We move like they do."

By moonset, the patrol was deep in the mountains. There was grass here for Indian ponies, and food in plenty—groves of oak trees heavy with acorns, clumps of mescal and Spanish dagger. There was everything but water, and Jess knew where to find that.

"I followed a deer in here once, a few months back," he explained to Nantahe as they rode. "There's a narrow canyon back there—you can barely see the mouth for the brush. But there's a little spring, and a lot of Indian sign. I got out in a hurry."

"That sounds right. Show us."

It was almost dawn before Jess saw the jagged entrance to the canyon silhouetted against the stars. "There," he whispered. He was trembling, partly from the early-morning chill, but mostly from excitement.

"We'll leave the horses here," Nantahe said. "You come on, and No-say. Deltche, bring the lieutenant and tell him we're scouting the *ranchería.*"

Deltche leaned in the saddle and caught Nantahe's arm.

"You take this *pinda lickoyi,*" he growled, pointing at Jess, "and leave me to hold horses? You shame me."

Nantahe stiffened, but he didn't pull away.

"I know you'll bring the patrol when we need them," he said. Then, softly, "And the white-eye has the right."

Slowly, Deltche drew back his hand. The other three dismounted, passing him the reins of their horses, and he turned back up the trail without a word. Nantahe watched him disappear into the darkness, then shrugged and motioned to Jess and No-say. Together, they started toward the hostile camp.

Jess thought himself a good tracker, but he found that he was noisy and clumsy beside the Apaches. He stayed close to Nantahe, while No-say moved off to one side, flitting from shadow to shadow until Jess lost him completely. Then he was suddenly back, crouching beside Nantahe.

"One guard," he breathed. "He's drunk. Maybe sign of thirty ponies."

"No-say, take the guard. Bring the patrol straight in when they get here." Nantahe's whisper hardly carried the few inches to Jess. "We'll go in now."

"That's crazy. You better wait," No-say protested, but Nantahe gestured impatiently. The other scout shrugged and drew his knife, then faded into the darkness again.

Nantahe gave him a few seconds, then unslung his Army Springfield and started forward. Jess followed, the Sharps clutched in sweating hands, his heart hammering with an emotion new to him. If No-say had seen evidence of thirty ponies, there must be many more hostiles here than the band he had tracked—and they felt perfectly safe.

Within the canyon, the cliff curved away to the left, forming a natural amphitheater. Branch-and-sapling shelters were scattered across its floor. Back against the rock itself, horses pawed restlessly in a brush corral. Jess paused, peering toward the camp, until a strong hand clamped down on his wrist.

"Hurry," Nantahe panted. "Day comes."

Jess threw a startled look at the sky. He hadn't noticed the gradual graying, but the stars were pale now and visibility was increasing by the minute. He tried to move quietly, but Nantahe half-dragged him past the *rancheria* and farther up the canyon, to a pile of boulders fallen from the overhanging cliff.

"Here." Nantahe threw himself flat behind the rocks and began laying out heavy copper cartridges for his Springfield. "Get ready," he told Jess. "This is their way out. They come here when—"

He stopped. In the village, a dog barked. Others joined in. Heads appeared at the entrance to one of the *jacales*. A man's voice shouted something, and suddenly running Apaches were everywhere. From the mouth of the canyon came a rising crackle of shots. Jess caught glimpses of a thin line of troopers weaving its way toward the village.

Apaches took cover among the *jacales* and fired at the patrol. Others tore down the walls of the corral, sending the panicked horses flying down the canyon toward the attackers. Under cover of the dust and confusion, a swarm of warriors broke for the rocks where Jess and Nantahe waited.

The crack of a carbine almost at his elbow startled Jess out of his trance. Nantahe fired again, and one of the closest hostiles slammed backward into the men behind him. The others hesitated in confusion. Nantahe methodically kicked the spent casing out of the Springfield and closed the breechblock on a fresh round.

The old Sharps came up almost of its own accord, steadying on a tall warrior running, stark naked, toward the rocks, a revolver in his fist. With his finger tight on the trigger, Jess froze. The realization that he held a man in his sights, a living man whom he wanted to kill, struck him with numbing force. Then he remembered what he had found at the ranch, and his finger closed in a smooth, effortless pull.

The Apache spun around and fell. Before the body hit the ground, Jess was feeding another shell into his rifle, firing with the same steady efficiency as Nantahe, but with less accuracy because his eyes were blinded by tears.

It was over before full daylight. The stampede had gained the hostiles enough time so that a few reached the heights. They pinned down Jess and Nantahe while those still trapped in the canyon swarmed up the sheer walls. Most escaped, but they escaped on foot, leaving behind their belongings and nine dead. The prisoners were six silent women, one of them badly wounded, and a young boy who stared back at his captors with fearless black eyes. The patrol had three wounded. One trooper and one Apache scout had been killed.

"He was a brave man. Maybe the Army can get his people a pension."

Nantahe knelt beside the body of Deltche. A bullet had caught the scout near the temple and torn out the back of his head. Nantahe looked up at Jess and smiled grimly.

"If he'd lived, one of us would have killed the other."

Jess turned away. There was a crawling sickness inside him, but worse was the sudden sense of being lost. Before the battle, he had had a purpose. Now there was nothing to hold on to but a memory he couldn't face.

"What now, son?" Callahan's soft voice asked the question Jess had been dreading. "We'll take you back to the fort, soon as we've burned this place. Did your pa have any people near here?"

Jess shook his head. "We had some kin back in Tennessee, but Pa didn't get on with them." He paused, rubbed a hand across his eyes. "I reckon I'll stay on at the place. It's mine, now, and Pa set a lot of store by it."

Callahan started to protest, but Nantahe rose from his place and came over.

"He did well in the fight, Nan-tan. You ought to make him a scout."

The lieutenant frowned. "You know I can't do that, Nantahe. The regulations say a man's got to be eighteen years old."

"I wasn't. I was already sergeant by my seventeenth summer."

"But you're an Apache," Callahan explained. "The rules are different for you."

Nantahe shrugged. Then he saw Jess, who had turned to listen, his face showing hope for the first time since they'd met.

"Enlist him as an Apache, then," Nantahe said.

He extended his hand. Jess hesitated, reached out gingerly. As he grasped Nantahe's hand, he knew he'd passed some sort of divide, that his life would be forever different because of that one gesture. Nantahe smiled.

"Say he's my brother," he said.

CHAPTER 3

The clouds blew away in a gusty dawn, leaving behind them a sea of mud that clung stubbornly to a man's boots or a horse's hooves. Looking beyond the mud, beyond the checkered fields of the Toyah Valley, Faver pointed toward the mountains rising mistily to the south.

"We'd better head southeast. If you keep gallopers and flankers out wide, we ought to hear some news before we get very far."

Lieutenant Miller eyed Faver uncertainly. He had ridden in the night before, at the head of a column of sleepy troopers from Fort Davis. He was young, not more than a year out of West Point, Faver guessed, and his carefully tended dragoon moustache didn't completely hide his inexperience.

"There can hardly be a trail after that rain, Mr. Faver. How can you tell which way to go?"

"It's the shortest way to the border," Faver said. He thought a moment. "Then, too, Apaches on the run will generally make for high country. That's the route I'd take if you were after me."

"I see."

Miller's tone was cold, and Faver looked at him sharply. Major Randall had spent an hour briefing the lieutenant before the train pulled out, and it would be interesting to know what Randall had said. Faver suspected the conversation hadn't been confined to Apaches.

Abruptly, Miller nodded. "Very well. You know your men, I'm sure." He turned, voice rising to a shout. "Sergeant Breymann, fall in the detail. Column of twos. Let's move out."

Within a few miles, the character of the country began to change. The irrigated farmland played out into low, rolling prairie covered with coarse grass. Gradually, the slopes grew steeper, the gullies lacing their flanks cut more deeply into the rocky soil, and

the column rode into badlands studded with mesquite and creosote bush.

Faver rode point, a quarter-mile ahead of the troop. As the
mud was left behind, he made short casts to either side of the line
of march, hoping to cut a fresh trail. He'd done it all before. It
almost seemed that this was another routine patrol from Fort
Apache, that the mountains now rising close ahead were the Ara-
vaipas, that Nantahe and the other scouts were the hunters, not
the quarry.

The morning was well along when a lone trooper topped a rise
to the west, sighted the column, and spurred his lathered horse
down to meet it. Faver cantered back as the man drew rein beside
Lieutenant Miller.

"Private Ames reporting, sir. Beg to report horses run off in the
night. A rancher down Ninemile Draw lost five head from his
corral."

Faver cut in close. "How far?" he asked. Miller shot him an annoyed glance, but nodded for the soldier to answer.

" 'Bout three miles southwest, sir." The private looked virtuous.
"I done just like the lieutenant said—told them it was Army business and not to do anything 'til we got there."

Miller nodded. "Well done, Ames. Fall in." He looked at Faver
with raised eyebrows. "Well, Mr. Faver, it seems that you guessed
right."

"It wasn't a guess, Lieutenant."

"We'll see." Miller raised his voice. "Column—trot! Follow me!"

The ranch house and its cluster of outbuildings lay on a grassy
bench above the flood channel of Ninemile Draw. The foreman
listened skeptically to Lieutenant Miller's explanation of their errand, then led the officer and Faver across the wagon yard to the
corral.

"This here's the place," he said. He was a small man, coming
barely to Faver's shoulder, and his wrinkled face was set in a quiz-
zical half-smile. "Didn't even hear the dogs bark. Guess maybe
my boys tracked things up some."

Faver looked sourly at the ground around the gate. It had been
trampled into slush by hooves and high-heeled boots.

"Guess they did. Wait here, Lieutenant, if you will."

Without waiting for a reply, he moved off in a long curve that took him into the brush behind the corral. He took it slowly, watching the ground, reaching once to touch the surface of a displaced stone. Finally, he retraced his route for ten or twenty yards, careful to step in the tracks he'd made. He stood there for a moment, looking thoughtfully at the long ridge of mountains to the south, then turned and walked back to the gate.

Miller had been watching with growing impatience. "Very impressive," he snapped. "Perhaps you'll honor us with your conclusions."

"Missing a lariat, most likely," Faver said to the ranch foreman.

"Well, they was somebody in the barn. Could have taken a lariat, easy enough."

"They did." Faver looked at the lieutenant. "Three horses went out of here in a bunch, just after the rain stopped. They went due south, across the draw. A lone horse headed southwest, and another went almost straight west."

The foreman spat on the ground, and his smile widened a bit.

"Shoot, son, we knew that. We were getting ready to follow those three that went south, when your soldier-boy stopped us."

"We'll take over," Miller said. "They're only a few hours ahead, and they aren't hiding their trail. Come on, Faver, let's ride."

He whirled and took a long stride back toward the waiting patrol. Faver's soft voice stopped him.

"Lieutenant? That's what Nantahe expects you to do."

"What?" Miller demanded. He stared at Faver. "I fail to see the humor. The Apaches have been careless, and you're wasting precious time."

Faver grinned. "Apaches are never careless. They roped the horses together, and one man—Nantahe, probably—took them south. He'll drop off someplace where his tracks won't show, then cut across to meet the others."

"On foot?" Miller snorted, but his face showed a hint of uncertainty. "Nonsense."

"It's a simple trick, Lieutenant," Faver explained patiently. "The horses will drift on downhill, probably with a few knife cuts to help them along, until they get tangled up in something. Nantahe figures you'll follow them. By the time you backtrack, the Apaches will pick up half a day."

"But of course the hostiles didn't realize they'd have a master tracker like yourself on their trail."

The officer's voice was heavy with scorn. Faver merely nodded. "That's right. You hunt Apaches with Apaches, Lieutenant, and the best scouts God ever made are either out ahead of us or on that damned train."

Faver stopped suddenly, frowned.

"But Nantahe should have known I'd be here."

"Maybe he knew," Miller said. "Maybe that's why he isn't hiding his trail."

Faver's eyes narrowed. For an instant, his face set in an expression that made Miller instinctively drop a hand to his holster flap. Then the scout caught himself and looked impassively at Miller.

"Suit yourself, Lieutenant. I'll be with the patrol when you're ready."

He strode away. Before he'd covered twenty yards, Miller caught him.

"You lead the way, Faver." The cavalryman still looked shaken, but his mouth was a tight line. "But, by God, you'd better be right."

The single trail to the southwest ran straight for five or six miles, then curved gradually back to the left. A second trail joined it, and there were two horses angling back toward the south. Just before dark, Faver picked out a third track, the prints of a man in moccasins joining the riders and moving thereafter at a long lope beside one of the horses.

Miller dismounted and dropped to one knee to work out the signs for himself. When he looked up, his eyes held a grudging respect.

"You were quite right, Mr. Faver." It wasn't exactly an apology, but Faver figured it was about as close as Miller would come. "Now, if we press on at the trot—"

"—you'll end up with a bunch of dead horses," Faver interrupted. "The Apaches have about four hours on us. They'll keep a steady pace all night, taking turns in the saddle, or running at the stirrup to rest their mounts. You can't catch them in a stern chase."

A quick flush sprang to Miller's cheeks. He opened his mouth to speak, closed it, and swallowed once.

"What do you suggest?" he asked.

Faver grinned at him.

"I suggest you dismount the detail and let them eat, while we look at that map of yours. If I'm right, it's the last rest we'll get for a while."

Sixty miles west of where the patrol lay, the Rio Grande ran almost due south to Stilwell's Crossing. Then the river swung eastward in a great, sweeping curve until it flowed north again through sheer-walled canyons. Beyond the river was Mexico. Within its bend, Miller's map showed a land of rugged mountains and grim, rocky desert.

"Water," Faver said. "Even Apaches need water." He looked up in the light of a flickering squad fire. "Old Chan-desi rode this country with Victorio. Where will he go for water?"

There was a silence. Then Sergeant Breymann cleared his throat diffidently. He was a stocky, moonfaced German who looked as little like a cavalryman as anybody Faver had ever seen, but he'd been in service a lot of years, and Faver had been pleasantly surprised that Miller showed sense enough to include him in the discussion.

"Ranches or line camps are near most of the waterholes. They will not attack a ranch?"

"No," Faver said decisively. Neither Nantahe nor Chan-desi were likely to look for that kind of trouble. Chicuelo, maybe, but Nantahe should be able to keep him under control. Faver shook off the nagging thought that Nantahe should have controlled him at the train.

"They'll be running," he said. "And they aren't hostiles. Not yet."

Miller raised his eyebrows momentarily, but didn't comment. Instead, he looked at the map, then at Breymann.

"Panther Spring," he said. "Sergeant?"

Breyman nodded quickly. "Of course, sir. It will be known to one of Victorio's men."

"Panther Spring?" Faver asked.

"It's on the north flank of the Chisos Mountains." Miller spread out the map, touched a spot deep within the bend of the river. "Maybe twenty miles from the border. It's an old Apache campsite."

"Will it be covered?"

"By troops?" Miller shook his head. "It isn't that important, usually. We could telegraph for patrols, or maybe the county sheriff, to cover the area between there and the border, but we could probably reach the spring ahead of anyone else."

Excitement had been creeping into Miller's face and voice as he spoke. Now he stopped and looked suddenly at Faver.

"Anyone except the Apaches," he amended. "If they're moving as fast as you say—"

He broke off as Faver came to his feet.

"They'll be swinging wide at every sign of people. If you push the detail straight through, you might beat them there." Faver shrugged. "Anyway, it's the only chance you've got."

Miller smiled in answer. "Then we'd better take it. Sergeant, mount the troop."

It was another night march, a forced march with no rest and men falling asleep in the saddles, the sliding thud of a heavy body striking the ground, weary cursing and catcalls as a trooper struggled back to his mount. It was a halt to boil coffee past midnight, glowing coals scattered by the toe of a cavalry boot, a quick splash of dirt from an entrenching tool.

"Mount up. Mount up. They're as tired as we are"—though Faver knew that wasn't true. "Push 'em. Push 'em 'til they drop."

They kicked on with the dawn coming on their left hand, among century plants that loomed out of the dark and bushel-basket-size clumps of buffalo grass. The sky lightened and the sun shouldered above the mountains. The morning heat of the desert clamped down, setting mirages to dancing in the distance. Gradually the ghostly peaks of the Chisos range rose and drew nearer, until they stretched like a gray-blue rampart across the detail's path and Panther Spring lay just ahead.

"Recommend you spread the men out," Faver said. "We'll flank them if they try to fight."

Miller frowned. The long ride had left its mark on the lieutenant. Neither his battered uniform nor his bristly and bleary-eyed face suggested the young West Pointer who'd met Faver at the train.

"We might be ahead of them. What if they double back?"

"We'll hold the spring and wait," Faver answered. "They'll be headed back toward your patrols, and their horses won't go much farther without water."

Miller nodded absently.

"Very well. Sergeant Breymann!"

The sergeant spurred up from the rear of the column. "Sir?"

"Deploy the men as foragers. And warn them to keep awake. This may be the finish."

The spring rose at the head of a rocky draw that slashed through the lower slopes of the Chisos Mountains. The land to the north was a series of parallel ridges, low and barren, alternating with cactus-covered flats. In the shelter of one of the ridges, the patrol shook itself out into a thin battle line. Faver rode ahead and Miller brought the troop on, still pressing hard.

They were crossing the last ridge when Faver reined up suddenly, signaling Miller to halt the patrol.

"Fresh tracks, fresh droppings," he called. He slipped from the saddle, kneeling as Miller rode up.

"Maybe twenty minutes old," Faver said. "We just missed jumping them."

Miller shaded his eyes and studied the mouth of the draw.

"Maybe we'd better dismount here and go in on foot. If they're still in there—"

Something struck the rocks two yards to Faver's left, glancing off with a wicked whine. He threw himself flat, hitching his carbine sling around as the crack of a rifle echoed from the rocks above the spring. The lieutenant piled off his horse and took cover beside him, pistol in hand.

"They're in there, all right." Faver rolled onto his side and grinned up at Miller. "Now all we have to do is get them out."

CHAPTER 4

Breymann brought the men up dismounted and hustled them into cover behind the ridgeline. A second shot sent rock fragments flying as he slid down beside Faver and the lieutenant.

"Sergeant, take two men and occupy that knob to the left." Miller was at home now, and the orders came crisply. "Give us covering fire. I'll—"

He stopped at a sudden gesture from Faver. A moment later, the sound of hoofbeats carried to the ridge. Through a gap in the rocks, a brown horse appeared. Carrying double, it plunged uphill in a desperate gallop.

"Fire!" Miller came to his knees, shouting to the troopers. "Fire! They're—uh!"

His yell ended in a startled grunt as Faver's arm snaked up and hauled him to the ground. A bullet plowed into the slope in front of them, and two more screamed off the rocks nearby. Moments later, a second horse burst from the draw. It disappeared into the rocks above the spring, its rider untouched by a scattering of shots from the troopers.

"Come on!" Miller sprang to his feet, waving violently for the horse-holders. "At the double! Let's move."

Faver was already mounted and down the slope, but instead of following the Apaches, he rode slowly toward the spring. When the patrol pounded up behind him, he was waiting within the mouth of the draw.

"What's wrong?" Miller demanded. "They're just ahead. We can get them, even if they did get to the water."

"They didn't."

Faver's voice was flat, tired. He swung down from his horse and tethered the animal loosely to a bush.

"We didn't beat them here, but we were close. Back there are the shell casings where one of them shot at us, and here's where they took the horses up the bank. They never got to the spring."

Miller followed Faver's pointing finger, took a moment to understand. "It's twenty miles over the mountains to the Rio Grande," he said slowly. "The Apaches will never make it on those mounts."

Faver nodded. "You might as well—" Then he stopped and started over. "I suggest the lieutenant water and rest the horses before we follow the hostiles."

"Thank you, Mr. Faver," Miller said formally. He turned in the saddle. "Sergeant, dismount the detail for watering. We move again in half an hour."

Lieutenant Miller paced restlessly during the halt, while his men sprawled near exhaustion on the grass. Faver hunkered against the bank and watched them through half-closed lids. The men were tired, but the rangy troop horses, watered now and grazing on the bluestem grass that grew thickly in the ravine, could go on any time. They were bony and ewe-necked, their manes tangled and their ankles swollen from the thorns of cactus and lechuguilla, but in the end they would run down the well-fed work mounts the Apaches had stolen. Endurance would tell the story, and water.

Water. Faver closed his eyes. Water was life here, as it was in Arizona. Once before, Faver had thought Nantahe was going out, and the reason had been water.

Faver first heard of it when Al Sieber, the shambling chief of scouts, had awakened him early one morning.

"Nantahe's gone," he'd said without preamble.

Faver sat up on his cot and rubbed sleep from his eyes. He'd grown in the two years since he'd met the patrol and Nantahe, grown both in body and in experience. He'd had a good teacher.

"Yeah? Gone where?"

Sieber shrugged. "If I knew, I wouldn't need you. The other scouts aren't talking, but it's something special. Something bad." He waited while Faver thought that over, then added, "I think you better find him."

"Yeah." Faver swung his legs off the cot and reached for his clothes. "I guess I'd better."

North and east of Fort Apache, back in the White Mountains, there was a canyon where a cold, narrow stream ran among stands of pine and cedar. Nantahe's clan, the In-the-Rocks People of the Chiricahua, had lived there years before. They were gone now, but there was still a broken rock dam across the stream, and a series of grassy terraces where women had planted corn, and hollows worn in the soft rock near the stream where the corn had been ground into meal. Nantahe had shown Jess the place once during a hunting trip. If the Apache had something to think out, that was where he'd go.

Faver rode into the canyon in late afternoon. The sheer walls were already deep in shadow, and a chill breeze stirred the surface of the stream. Faver faintly smelled the smoke of burning cedar on the wind. At the bend above the village site, he found Nantahe's pony, hobbled and grazing. Faver dismounted, gave his horse a leisurely rubdown, and turned him out to graze. Carrying his saddle and blanket roll, he walked in on Nantahe's camp.

The Apache sat cross-legged before a little fire. His hands were folded across the gourd canteen he held in his lap, but his rifle leaned against a rock within easy reach. Back in the shadows, Faver saw a lean-to of freshly cut branches and a neat stack of firewood. It looked as if Nantahe meant to stay awhile.

Nantahe made no sign as Faver dropped his gear and squatted beside the fire. Faver reached out lazily, pulled a grass stem, and stuck it between his teeth. He waited. Nantahe would talk when he was ready.

After a time, Nantahe took a pull from the canteen, then passed it across to Faver. Jess drank, grimacing at the raw bite of the mescal. Nantahe looked at him for the first time.

"At first, I was going to do this the Apache way—build a sweat-bath, fast, pray for guidance," he said. He took the gourd and tipped it up again. "Now I think I'll try the white man's way and get drunk."

"Sieber thinks you've turned *bronco*. I don't."

"No?" Nantahe almost smiled. Then he shook his head. "You know about the water?"

"Yeah."

Everyone knew about the water. White settlers on the borders of the Fort Apache Reservation had been taking water for irrigation, water that Apache farmers needed desperately. The chiefs had appealed to the Indian Bureau, and the case had gone up through channels. Just a few days ago, a decision had been handed down: under the law, Indians could not hold water rights.

"Will your crops be hurt, brother?" Faver asked. "I didn't know you were such a farmer."

Nantahe might not have heard. "They leave us nothing," he said softly in Apache. "They take our land and our water and our honor and there is no one we can trust."

"How about Crook?" Faver demanded. "How about Callahan and the other soldiers? You've fought beside them. Can't you trust them?" He paused for a long moment, then asked very quietly, "Can you trust me, brother?"

Nantahe looked at him a moment, finally lowered his eyes. He started to take another drink, then changed his mind and set the gourd aside.

"A lot of the People don't like the scouts, Jess. They call us traitors."

"I know. But the renegades kill Apaches as well as whites."

"They fight!" The words came from Nantahe with unexpected violence. "I've always thought this way was better. It may not be as good as the old days, but at least the People can live in peace."

Faver didn't know how to answer. He'd ridden with Nantahe for two years, but he'd never realized the pressures, the pull of the old ways, that acted on the Apache scouts. He'd been aware of a watchful reserve somewhere behind Nantahe's friendship, and now he knew what it meant.

"But peace is no good," Nantahe went on, almost to himself. "It's no good if we have nothing left, if laws are only for the whites."

"It'll get better, Nantahe. When the wild ones, the cut-offs, are whipped, there'll be real peace. Then things will change."

For a moment, Nantahe stared at him as if he stood on the far side of some great canyon. Then the Apache nodded slowly.

"I hope so."

"It'll change," Faver promised. He managed a grin and reached across for the gourd canteen. "Meantime, I like your first idea. Let's get drunk."

And they'd gotten drunk and gone tomcatting around Old Man Turtle's wickiup, where his three daughters lived, and Old Man Turtle had almost shot them before he found out who they were.

That had been six years ago—six years of grinding, bloody war. Faver had predicted that things would be different, and so they were. The scouts were on their way to prison, and Nantahe and the others were out in the hills, hunted like animals, land and rank and honor gone. Faver wondered grimly if Nantahe remembered the night in the canyon as clearly as he did.

"Prepare to mount. Mount! By the walk, yo-o!"

The trail led upward, past the barren, brown lower slopes and into a fringe of juniper. The Apaches' horses were tiring, and the rocks were flecked with their blood, showing that they were being mercilessly lashed.

"We'd better spread out," Faver advised. "They may leave the horses and hole up someplace until we pass them."

Miller scanned the slope ahead, frowning. "They're walking into a trap. It's a dead end, if they keep on in this direction."

Faver paused and looked at the lieutenant questioningly. "Are you sure? I wouldn't expect Chan-desi to get lost."

"Well, he's made a bad guess this time. They might double back on foot, but we should get them if they do." Miller rode in silence for a minute, then turned to Faver again. "Suppose we corner them. Will they fight?"

Faver shook his head. Running was one thing, even killing the sentry during the escape. A stand-up fight with a cavalry troop was something else, when the best a man could do was take a few troopers along on the long ride.

"I doubt it. If we don't get trigger-happy, I think they'll give up."

"I hope so, Faver. I really do."

The trail took them over a pass, into a basin surrounded by pine-clad peaks. Miller spread the patrol still wider, trying to watch all sides for an ambush, but the tracks drove straight across the hollow and into a narrow defile.

"This is it," Miller said. "We have them." He stood in his stirrups. "Stevens and Cass, take the right flank. Watson and Schwartz, cover the left. Stay on the banks, and see that nothing gets past us."

Faver and the lieutenant in the lead, the patrol plunged into the mouth of the gully. Its floor sloped steadily downward, and its dirt banks gave way to walls of sheer rock that soon rose high above the riders. Faver slowed the pace, knowing that any turn, any boulder, might hold an ambush. This was no ordinary draw. It was an outlet for the basin behind them, a single opening that funneled water to someplace. Before they reached that place, the Apaches would have to make a stand.

The walls closed in until the column had to move in single file. Then there was a final turn and the draw widened into a rock chute, forty yards long and arrow-straight, its sides scored and polished by rushing water. A horse stood uncertainly in the mouth of the chute, and another lay nearby with its legs doubled under it. Beyond, there was nothing but blue sky.

"They must be here," Miller cried. Echoes mocked him. "Flankers!"

"Nobody up here, Lieutenant," came a voice from almost overhead.

Faver dismounted and worked his way to the lip of the chute. Below him, the cliff fell away for a sheer four hundred feet, then stepped down in stages to the desert floor. Near the bottom, just coming through the last part of the climb, were three tiny figures. Looking down, back braced against the cold rock, he could make out a network of handholds a man might follow if he were desperate enough.

"There they are, Lieutenant. Want to try and follow them?"

Miller came to look and swore bitterly. "Outsmarted again!" He slammed a fist into his open palm. "It's all my fault. I never imagined—"

"No reason why you should. Now you know."

The officer turned from the edge and took the bridle of the abandoned horse, absently rubbing the animal's neck with his free hand. The horse made an odd moaning sound and pitched to its knees. Miller's hand came away red with blood.

The lieutenant stared in shock for an instant. Then he snatched a carbine from one of the troopers and pumped a shot down toward the Indians. Six hundred yards away, shooting downhill in the uncertain light of late afternoon, he had no chance, but the sound carried. The Apaches paused and looked back. One of them raised his arm and waved.

It was Nantahe, Faver knew, just as he was sure Nantahe knew who was looking down on him. They had played a game, with move and countermove, and Nantahe was the better player. Long before the patrol could retrace its path in the coming darkness, the fugitives would cross the border into Mexico, where the Army couldn't follow. Nantahe had won, and Faver wondered if there would be another round.

"They stabbed the horses." Miller's voice was blurred with fatigue and disbelief. "This one's hamstrung. There was no reason for it, none at all."

"To an Apache, there is," Faver said. "He won't let anything fall into enemy hands. If he has to leave it, he'll see nobody else can use it."

At least, that was how the bitter-enders were, the ones who would never give up. Nantahe and the others were different. Or they had been.

Faver looked down at the sweep of land within the river's curve. Off to the south, the way the Apaches had gone, he saw the glow of a tiny fire and a drift of white smoke. A line shack, maybe, or someone's camp. For the first time, he felt a nagging sense of worry.

"I think we'd better get down there," he said.

Getting down wasn't easy. Neither the horses nor the men were in shape for another night march. Miller, much against his will, was forced to stop in the basin for precious hours. He had the patrol up and moving again long before dawn, stumbling in darkness toward the spot where the Apaches had last been seen.

Faver stayed at the head of the column, tried to pick the easiest path. There was still a chance—barely a chance—they could somehow intercept Nantahe. If not, it was all over. Standing orders forbade American troops to enter Mexico, and those orders included Faver.

He'd ridden many patrols where the chase had ended at the border, but this one was different. This time, he wasn't sure he could let it go.

The patrol was still a few miles short of its goal when Faver suddenly reined in.

"Listen."

Miller raised his head, stiffened as he heard it, too—a distant popping, muffled and distorted by echoes and distance, almost drowned by the small noises of the night.

"That's gunfire."

Faver nodded. "Off to the southwest, I think." He stood in the stirrups, as if that would help him see across the hills. "There was a campfire over there. The Apaches must have seen the smoke."

"You think it's them?"

"It's them. Let's move."

They picked up the smoke again just after sunup. Miller pulled the scattered troopers together, brought them fast across the hills, and threw them over the last ridge at a gallop.

In the depression below, half a dozen men were preparing breakfast around a small fire. They scrambled for their guns as the patrol poured down on them. Then they recognized the uniforms and relaxed, standing sheepishly as the soldiers pulled up and dismounted. A tall, gray-haired man came out to meet Miller.

"Sure glad to see you boys. I figured we'd have to walk out of here. I'm Ed Hollowell, the county sheriff."

Hollowell's men drew together around the fire, seeming almost reluctant to mix with the troopers. One of them leaned back on his bedroll. He had a bloody bandage around his shoulder. Another figure lay motionless a few yards away, covered by a poncho.

"We heard the shots, Sheriff. What happened here?"

"Your Apaches jumped us. We'd got the word on the telegraph and were out looking for them, but some knothead"—he transferred his gaze to one of the deputies, who hastily looked away—"went to sleep on guard. They run off our horses, but we got one of them." •

Two long strides took Faver to the body on the ground. He drew back the poncho and looked down at the face of Chan-desi. Dead, the old man looked frail and peaceful. Gently, Faver replaced the covering.

"He was carrying this." Hollowell held up an Army-model Colt's pistol. "They were leading out the horses when Sam, there, woke up and hollered. We got the one, but the other two mounted up and got away. And our horses are scattered from hell to breakfast out there."

Faver didn't turn from the body. "Who fired first?" he asked.

"Well—I reckon we did. It was kind of confused, but Russ was hit right at the end. We almost had them all."

Faver could see how it had been: the Apaches, running for the river, safe. The posse would seem easy pickings, a chance to ride into Mexico with dignity—and, for Nantahe, a few more points in the game. Then Chan-desi was dead, and it wasn't a game anymore. Faver hadn't been sure what Nantahe would do when he reached Mexico, but he knew now.

"I'll bury him," he said.

Hollowell cleared his throat. "No, I reckon we'll take him back with us, show the folks here we aren't wasting their tax money."

Faver straightened, his jaw set, but the lieutenant spoke first. "The Apache was a government scout, Sheriff. We'd like to take charge of his body."

"This is my county, mister. I've got jurisdiction."

"I see." Miller paused thoughtfully. "Sheriff, I wish I could detail some men to help round up your horses, but my orders are to follow the Apaches." He turned away, then looked back. "By the way, will you want a copy of my report for your records?"

Hollowell's face reddened. He glared at Miller. After a moment, he turned the glare on Faver, but found no help there. Abruptly, he wheeled and stalked off without a word.

"Sergeant Breymann," Miller called. "Send out a party to locate the sheriff's mounts. And detail two men for a burial party."

The sergeant saluted and moved off.

"Thanks," Faver said.

Miller shrugged. "My job. Your job is tracking Apaches. Let's see you track some."

The trail led straight south, clear and easy to follow, across the barren hills to the banks of the Rio Grande. In the mud along the water's edge, Faver found the deep-cut tracks of two horses.

"That's it," Miller said. "We've lost them."

Faver looked across at the far bank. Nantahe would avenge Chan-desi's death; Apache law demanded it. Now Faver had to go after him, and Randall's orders were the least of his reasons.

"I haven't lost them." He swung back into the saddle. "I'm going to bring them back."

"But my orders—"

"I'm not under your command," Faver said. "I guess I'm not under anybody's command. You going to stop me?"

Slowly, Miller shook his head. "You escaped," he said. "But if you cross that river, you're through as a scout. Randall will see to that."

"Don't blame him a bit, Lieutenant."

He pressed his knees into his pony's sides, guiding the animal down into the shallows. Halfway across, with water lapping cold around his thighs, he turned in the saddle and looked back. Miller and the patrol were already lost to sight among the willow breaks, and with them had gone the only life Faver knew.

Randall might see him drummed out of the scouts, but the days of the scouts were ending anyway. Every tribe, excepting only the Apaches, had been smashed by ceaseless campaigning and chained on reservations. With Geronimo's surrender, the Apaches were beaten as well. There would be trouble for years with renegades, with outcasts who could make no peace, could only kill until they died—but the Apache wars were over, and a part of Faver's life had ended with them.

He clucked to the restless horse and the animal pushed on against the fingers of the current. As Nantahe's handshake years ago had been a watershed in his life, Faver knew that this river marked a fresh one. Nantahe would never come in, never accept imprisonment. By crossing the river after him, Faver was opening a fresh contest with the Apache—a contest only one of them could survive.

CHAPTER 5

During the night, clouds rolled in from the north—dark clouds, heavy with rain. Faver awoke two hours before dawn. He lay quiet, his hand gripping the butt of his revolver under the rolled clothing he used as a pillow. He felt the stillness, the change from the steady southward breeze that had been blowing when he made camp, and he knew the change had awakened him.

He rolled out of his blankets, shivering as the first cold gust from the storm front reached him. Soon there would be rain, the driving, windswept rain of the desert country, washing out his chances of following Nantahe and Chicuelo. By daylight, there would be no trail.

Swiftly, Faver lashed the blankets into a tight roll and shoved them far back under the rocky overhang where he had camped. He added his saddle and saddlebags to the pile, then loosened the hobbles on his horse, giving the animal freedom to graze or to shelter from the rain. That done, he settled comfortably beneath the overhang, his carbine across his knees, and tried to think his way into Nantahe's mind.

The Apaches held all the cards now. Mounted on fresh horses and safe from immediate pursuit, they could simply disappear into the tortured canyon country of northern Mexico. They could live off the land, off the game and the agave plants that Ysun had provided for the Apache, until even Faver gave up the hunt.

They could do that if they chose, and many Apaches had done so rather than return to reservations north of the border. Faver didn't think that was the choice Nantahe and Chicuelo would make, though. They were fighters. Chicuelo had ridden with Cochise before becoming a scout. They had killed once, and they had lost Chan-desi. Sooner or later, they would hit back for that.

Faver couldn't follow them, but he could ride the ridges and canyons looking for them. He could watch and listen, and if they chose not to hide, he would hear of it. Meantime, he could only wait for the rain to stop, and for the hunch or instinct or hidden knowledge that would take him to the right place. His hat tilted over his eyes, his hands on the carbine, Faver waited.

He rode south again next day, across low, rocky ridges. Muddy water still swirled in a few of the draws, and he crossed a wagon road with fresh ruts cut deep in the red mud. He swung wide of the road and the *ranchos* along it, because he knew that was what Nantahe would do. Toward afternoon, he cut the trail of a large party of horsemen and stopped to examine the tracks.

There had been at least twenty horses, all of them shod, moving in a compact group. It looked as if a cavalry patrol had passed, so much so that Faver circled wide and found, as he expected, the tracks of a pair of flankers parallel to the main column. Watery sunlight glinted on something just off the line of march. Faver investigated and found the fragments of a shattered whiskey bottle.

"Huh," he grunted, half aloud. "Now, what kind of outfit—?"

He left the rest of the thought unspoken, but straightened to scan the nearby hills before he rode on.

By afternoon, he was climbing again, into a new range of mountains where cedar thickets lay dark along the slopes. The ranch country, with its clustered *jacales* wherever there was water, was behind him. The mountains looked wilder, more forbidding. They'd be a good place for anyone who wanted to hide.

Back in one of the canyons, Faver cut a narrow, well-worn trail. It might have been merely a game trail, but something about it didn't look quite right, and on impulse he turned to follow it. There must be people living back in the hills somewhere, and it might help him if he knew who they were.

The trail led into a side canyon where a trickle of water flowed, cold and probably spring-fed. Faver left his horse and went on cautiously. There were plentiful tracks of goats and burros and, not far in, a rock pen holding a few goats. Beyond that, Faver found a place where the canyon widened out. Watermelons and squash grew in a sandy patch by the stream, and a few withered cornstalks stood forlornly nearby. In the middle of the clearing was a hide-covered wickiup. Smoke rose lazily from its vent hole.

Faver found a vantage point in a clump of willows along the

stream and settled down to watch. After a time, an old Apache woman came outside. Singing softly, she dumped a lump of bread dough from the basket she carried, kneaded it into shape on a flat rock, and shoveled it into the domed adobe oven by her doorway. Faver watched patiently as she moved through other household chores and finally withdrew inside as darkness came. No one else had moved in or around the wickiup, and the woman hadn't seemed to be expecting company, though she did glance down the canyon once or twice.

Faver made a fireless camp back downstream that night, keeping a fitful watch over the trail. He'd known there were Apaches in the area, but it was anybody's guess how many and where. They might help Nantahe and Chicuelo, or they might consider the whole affair none of their business. That was about the best Faver could hope for.

Either way, Faver knew that the People would soon hear the whole story, would know who the strange white-eye was and what he wanted. Maybe it would be better to get his version in first.

When morning came, he rolled his blankets behind his saddle and rode boldly up the canyon. The woman was sitting beside her doorway, her head bent over the dress she was mending. She looked up as Faver dismounted. Her braided hair was almost white and her knuckles were gnarled with arthritis, but the eyes that peered at him were bright and alert in the wrinkled face.

"Good morning, Grandmother," Faver greeted her in Apache. She snorted.

"Good morning, white-eye who talks like an Apache and lies in the bushes spying on old women. Are you part of that scum from the hills, or are you running from the law?" She looked more closely at him. "Or are you another thing again?"

Faver laughed. "Well, until just now, I thought I was a scout. Can I sit down?"

"The ground is free." Then, as Faver started to sit, she gestured impatiently. "Unbit that scrawny horse first. I suppose you'll want something to eat."

Over a meal of kid stew and fried bread, Faver learned that the woman was called Juana, and that she'd been living in the area since the destruction of Victorio's band six years before. There were apparently a fair number like her, with the Mexican troops paying little attention to them as long as they didn't make trouble. Most didn't.

"There are always a few who'd rather steal than work," Juana said. "They run off a few sheep and call themselves warriors. If one stole a cow, he'd be Geronimo." She shrugged. "They aren't many. They kill each other off, or the *soldados* get them. But they'll even steal from an old woman!"

"A helpless old woman?" Faver asked, grinning at her sudden indignation.

Juana smiled a snaggletoothed smile.

"My grandson looks after me, and I have friends among the People." Her tone sharpened. "And even an old woman can pull a trigger. You remember that next time you come creeping around."

"I was looking for a man. Two men, rather. They can make more trouble than all your sheep-stealers put together."

Briefly, he told her the whole story—enough of it, anyway. There was no reason to lie. If the Apaches here were sympathetic to Nantahe and Chicuelo, he'd better know it from the start.

When he'd finished, Juana put her hand to her forehead.

"I knew you were trouble," she said. When Faver didn't speak, she went on. "I don't know anything, and I wouldn't tell if I did. The renegades mostly leave me alone. There are Mexican bandits who rob the mines, and soldiers who chase them, but they leave me alone, too. Why do I want to change any of that?"

She looked up at Faver.

"Most of the People will feel the same way. We live between the soldiers and the cut-offs. We don't get in anybody's way."

"I know," Faver said. "But tell your friends why I'm here. The word will get back to Nantahe and Chicuelo."

"*Muy loco*. They will kill you."

"Maybe."

Faver rose and brushed the dust from his knees. Without speaking again, he saddled and bridled his horse, then turned to face the old woman again.

"The Mexican soldiers don't bother you now. Suppose Nantahe and Chicuelo aren't willing to hide out, or to stick to rustling. If they kill people, do you think the soldiers will care which Apaches did it?"

He waited. When she didn't answer, he swung lightly into the saddle and kneed his pony around.

"Good-bye, Grandmother. Thanks for the meal. I'll see you again."

The old woman laughed bitterly. "If you live," she said.

On to the south, the hills ran out into broken desert. Beyond that, another range rose in a long hogback, its lower slopes breaking against a sheer rampart of cliff. There was no sign of life in all that stretch of land, and Faver reined in to consider. He was low on supplies. If necessary, he could live off the land as well as Nantahe, but it would be better to find a town or *rancho* where he could buy food and ask questions. From what Juana had said, it could be a long hunt.

He followed a draw off to the east, where the land seemed less arid. Eventually, the draw led him to a road, a pair of wagon ruts cut deeply into white dust. There were other tracks in the dust as well, the prints of ten or a dozen ponies. This time, most of the horses were unshod.

Faver followed the tracks, pausing to loosen the Springfield in its scabbard before he rode on. The horses had passed sometime the day before, he judged. He wasn't likely to ride up on the band that had made them, but he had an idea he'd better be ready, all the same.

He saw the farm ahead when the road crossed a rise. Without pausing, he rode on across the crest, then turned aside in the next draw. He tied his horse there and uncased a battered pair of field glasses, scrambling up the bank for a better look.

Two buildings came into focus, house and barn, with a well in the open yard between them. The inevitable cornstalks grew not far from the house, with melons and chilies spreading green between the rows. A stone corral stood empty beside the barn, and the door of the house was open.

Frowning, Faver returned to his horse. He half drew the carbine, then shoved it back again. Visitors didn't show up with gun in hand here, not if they wanted to stay alive.

He checked the cylinder of his revolver and settled the gun gently in its holster, leaving the flap open. Then he mounted and returned to the road. There was something wrong down there, in that quiet valley, and he had to find out what it was.

The tracks he'd been following split into three groups a few hundred yards short of the buildings. Five horses had stopped behind a thicket of brush, stood for a while, then gone straight in. The others had divided left and right to surround the place. Faver paused to read the signs, then rode on. As he came into the open, within sight of the empty windows, his muscles tightened involuntarily. He felt that he was being watched—maybe tracked in the sights of a rifle—though his sharpened senses told him it was only in his mind.

He dismounted before the house and stood for a moment, listening. There should have been chickens clucking, animals moving about in the barn, perhaps the sound of voices. There was nothing.

"*Buenos días,*" Faver called. "Is anyone here?"

He waited, then yanked the Springfield from its scabbard and walked toward the house. He could see now that the heavy wooden door was sagging inward, half torn from its hinges. The tracks told a story here, too—a confused story of horses coming in at a gallop, of running men and riderless mounts from the empty corral. On the ground and splattering up onto the lower part of the whitewashed wall was a broad stain dried rusty-red in the sun.

Faver kicked open the door with a crash that shattered the stillness. He went in fast and low, landed on one knee with the carbine cocked in his hands. The room was a shambles. It had apparently served as kitchen and living area. The rough wooden table was overturned, and fragments of broken dishes crunched under Faver's boots as he stood up.

A quick check showed that the pantry and cellar had been stripped of food. Almost everything else was wrecked. A domed adobe oven stood miraculously untouched in the kitchen and, from a tin plate on one wall, the peaceful face of a saint looked down.

Faver followed the painted gaze through the doorway into the second room. There he found the woman.

She had been young. Faver thought she had been pretty. Her body was spread-eagled on the rawhide bed, wrists and ankles lashed to the bedposts, and the things that had been done to her removed any doubt that this was Apache work.

Faver yanked a curtain from the tangle—white curtains, sewn

with small, careful stitches—and covered her. Then he went outside, leaned against the cool adobe wall, and retched until his throat was raw and his belly cramped with racking dry heaves.

When it ended at last, he drank from his canteen and wiped his mouth savagely. At least there had been no one to witness his shame, he thought, then laughed shortly as he recognized the feeling. Nantahe had taught him well. A man should hide his emotions, should show no sign of weakness. Faver drew a long breath and straightened. Maybe he didn't measure up to that standard.

He spent another twenty minutes checking out the house and barn. Except for the one bloodstain, he found hardly a trace of the others who had lived here. Among the jumbled tracks was the single print of a child's bare foot. Another place, there was a broad furrow where something had been dragged behind a horse. That was all, but it was enough.

Throughout his search, Faver watched for a sign that Nantahe or Chicuelo had been there. The old woman had spoken of renegades, and this could be their doing. He didn't really believe it, though. Rape and murder didn't square with her description of the cut-offs—unless something had happened to change them.

He took a last look around, the carbine dangling loosely in his hands. He'd found no tools, not even a hoe to scoop out a grave, and he was in a hurry now. If he were found here, it would lead to questions or worse. *Gringos* were seldom welcome along the border. He might never get a chance to explain his presence.

"I guess not," he said aloud.

He grasped the saddle horn to mount, then spun around abruptly, the Springfield coming into line almost of its own accord. His horse neighed and pawed the dust, but Faver stood frozen, listening.

The sound came again—a low, bleating moan like the cry of a newborn lamb. It came from the house. For a single shocked moment, Faver thought of the woman on the bed, and the hair prickled on the back of his neck. Then he shook off the idea and shoved through the door into the kitchen.

There were no more cries, but after a moment he heard a low rustling to his left. There was nothing there—nothing but empty shelves, a dented tin pail, the fragments of crockery, the big oven with its mouth blocked by a piece of sheet iron.

The oven. Faver took a long step and knocked away the brick holding the iron door in place. It fell with a clatter. Inside, resting on the ashes, was a bundle that gave out a thin wail of protest when he touched it.

"Oh, Lord," Faver whispered.

The child couldn't have been more than six months old. It was wrapped tightly in a knitted shawl. A piece of rag, probably soaked in milk, had been thrust into its mouth to keep it quiet. The woman must have had only moments to hide the baby.

Moments, followed by long hours made worse by the fear that the child would wake and cry, or would die before anyone came. It was a picture Faver would have trouble forgetting.

The baby was crying, and Faver turned, almost with relief, to the problems involved there. He knew there was no milk, so he dipped the rag in water and gave it to the child to suck. He stripped off the shawl and underclothes, and made a reasonable job of swaddling the boy—for it was a boy—in another scrap of curtain.

Outside, he rigged an Apache-style cradle from the shawl and looped it over his saddle horn, testing to be sure it would ride safely. The baby was still crying weakly, but there was nothing he could do about that. He mounted and urged his horse to a gallop, back up the wagon road the way he had come.

The trail of the raiders lay to the south, but it would have to wait. His resolve to stay away from people would have to wait, as well. He could only hope, if the child was to live, that the road would carry him to a town, and soon.

CHAPTER 6

Hours passed, and the afternoon drew into evening. Finally, the road crossed a crest and descended by a series of switchbacks into a valley. The valley was wide, greener than the surrounding countryside, cleft down the middle by a deep, rocky dry wash. In places along the valley floor, there were springs and seeps, choked in tangles of willow and river cane, and soon the wash was a creek with a respectable amount of water tumbling over its boulders.

The road was better here, and well-traveled side trails led off into the hills. Faver was tempted to turn aside, but he couldn't be sure of what he'd find at the other end. He'd tried earlier to give more water to the baby, but had failed to stop its thin crying. Now the child was quiet, and Faver didn't like that.

The town of La Morita stood on a flat-topped hill well above the flood-crest of the creek. Faver saw first the white stuccoed bell tower of the church, then the building itself, then the low tan and white *jacales* surrounding it. He kicked his horse into a trot up the grade. A few people gathered in the dusty street to watch his approach, but disappeared inside when he called to them. He rode through a street of closed doors to the broad, bare plaza in the middle of town.

The church took up the west side of the square, its tower frowning across at three tiny *cantinas* opposite it. A big, white-painted store with a wooden porch and a tin roof accounted for the north side, but it was the building on the south that interested Faver. It was long and low, with many doors opening onto the plaza. A Mexican flag hung limply beside one of the doorways, and a hand-painted sign identified it as the office of the *Comandante de Guardia Nacional*.

Faver reined in and dismounted. A crowd was collecting in front of the store, the people staring across at him. A woman came out onto the porch, a uniformed man by her side. After a moment, they were joined by another man, heavily bearded and unmistakably American. He said something to the officer, who shook his head and came quickly down the steps. He seemed to be in charge, and Faver started toward him. Then, surprisingly, the baby began to cry.

Faver hesitated, then went back and took the shawl holding the infant from the saddle horn. He turned, holding the squirming bundle awkwardly in both hands, to find himself confronting the Mexican officer.

The man was in his late twenties, Faver guessed, with a thin face and the high cheekbones of an aristocrat. He wore the collar facings of a captain. His lips were quirked in an unwilling smile at Faver's predicament, but his eyes were hard and questioning. He started to speak, but someone suddenly brushed past him and snatched at the baby.

"Paquito!" The woman from the porch—hardly more than a girl, Faver saw now—pressed the child to her breast. She unwrapped the shawl and held it up.

"Luis, this is Carla's shawl! It's Paquito! Where did this man find him?"

She wheeled and volleyed questions at Faver, speaking much faster than he could follow. He'd learned enough Spanish on the reservation to get by—more Apaches spoke Spanish than English— but he could only shake his head as the storm of words broke over him. When she paused for breath, he spoke quickly.

"He was at a *rancho,* maybe fifteen miles south of here. The stock had been run off, and there was nobody there except—"

He stopped. The girl was staring at him, lips parted, her eyes wide with fear and worry.

"There was nobody there," he said.

"That can't be! What about Carla and my uncle? They'd never leave Paquito, never! You're lying!"

"Estella. Be quiet." The captain took hold of her arm. "I'll see to this."

She jerked her arm away. "No! I have to know what happened. Make him tell!"

The crowd had worked its way across the street, growing larger as the news spread, until it almost surrounded Faver and the

others. It greeted the girl's last words with a low, ugly murmur.
The captain looked up quickly.

"*Madre de Dios,*" he muttered. Then, raising his voice, "This
is military business, not a circus. Go home, all of you. Sandoval,"
—to a soldier gawking from the barracks doorway—"get them out
of here."

The people began to drift away, reluctantly, pausing often to
look back, gathering in little whispering knots. Estella still looked
rebellious, and the captain turned on her.

"You, Estella. Paquito is crying. He must be fed. Take care of
him."

She still hesitated. Then the bearded American who Faver had
noticed before came forward, speaking gently to her.

"Capitán Ordoñez is right, *señorita*. Let him handle it. We'll
see that the truth comes out."

The girl shook her head in confusion. She bent over the child,
seeming to hear its cries for the first time.

"I gave him water," Faver said. "But I didn't have anything he
could eat, and I don't know—"

He broke off as her head came up. She gave him a scornful
look, then turned her back on him.

"I'll be back," she told the captain. Cradling the infant in her
arms, she went off toward the houses. The captain shook his head.

"It is the ranch of her aunt and uncle—her father's brother." He
seemed to be speaking more to himself than to Faver. "Her father
is dead."

Then he looked at Faver and his tone changed.

"I am Captain Luis Ordoñez of the *Guardia Nacional,* commandant of this district. And you?"

"Jess Faver."

Ordoñez raised his eyebrows at the brevity of the introduction.
His unhurried gaze took in the McClellan saddle on Faver's
mount, the Springfield carbine, the high-topped cavalry boots
Faver wore. His face was expressionless, but Faver could read
enough in the hard brown eyes. There was suspicion there—a
wariness extending, Faver suspected, to all *gringos* in the troubled border country.

"Perhaps you would step into my office, Señor Faver."

Ordoñez gestured abruptly to the watching soldier. "Sandoval, take care of the gentleman's horse."

Faver hesitated as the *soldado* came forward to take the bridle. Then he unstrapped the saddlebags and slung them over his shoulder, pulled the carbine from its boot. He nodded to Ordoñez. Before the captain could move, however, the bearded American quickly stepped up to Faver.

"I didn't really get to introduce myself." He extended a hand. "Braswell, Jonas Braswell. I run the store over there. 'Stella—the young lady—works for me."

Faver shook his hand. Braswell was perhaps an inch shorter than he was, and solidly built. His neatly trimmed hair and beard showed just a sprinkling of gray. He looked calm and comfortable. For a moment, looking at the easy smile, Faver had the idea he'd seen Braswell before, but he knew he must be wrong.

Still smiling, the trader turned to face Ordoñez.

"With your permission, I'd like to sit in while you talk to Mr. Faver. Maybe I can help out."

"This is military business."

"Of course. But Señorita Alvarado is my friend as well as my clerk. I feel responsible for her. And you might need an interpreter."

"Señor Faver's Spanish is adequate." Ordoñez was brusque, almost hostile. "My English is also sufficient. Now, if you will excuse us—"

Braswell shook his head sadly. "I'd hoped we wouldn't have to bother the *jefe político* with this little matter. But a foreigner in a questionable position is certainly his business."

The captain sighed and murmured something, then bowed toward the door.

"A pleasure to have you, Señor Braswell. Come."

The office seemed dark after the harsh glare of sunlight on the square. It held only a field desk, an iron stove, and a couple of extra chairs. A chromolithograph of the *Virgen de Guadelupe* hung on one wall, and a framed portrait of President Díaz in Army uniform on another.

Braswell claimed one of the chairs, and Ordoñez crossed to the stool behind the desk. Faver dumped his saddlebags in a corner and leaned the carbine against the wall beside them, then took the remaining chair.

"There was something you didn't wish to say before Señorita Alvarado," Ordoñez said without preamble. "What was it?"

"There was a dead woman at the ranch," Faver said. "She'd been"—he searched for the word in Spanish—"been violated."

Ordoñez glanced quickly at Braswell, then looked at Faver with narrowed eyes.

"Strange," he murmured. "Zamora's men are ruthless to their enemies, but the Alvarados were not enemies. In fact—"

He broke off, with another glance at Braswell. The trader started to say something, but Ordoñez held up a hand.

"Very well. It takes no great intelligence to see you've been a soldier. Report."

"Not a soldier," Faver said. But he reported, carefully and completely, beginning at the moment he'd first seen the Alvarado place. Ordoñez interrupted only once, to ask if the ashes where Faver found the baby had still been warm.

"A strange tale," he said at the end. He rested his chin on his clasped hands and smiled. "Why did Zamora send you?"

"Now, Captain—" Braswell began. Faver overrode him.

"I don't know any Zamora. I've told you how it happened."

He said it quietly, but there was a hard edge in his voice.

"Indeed? Then who do you suppose attacked the *rancho?*"

Faver hesitated for an instant, saw the captain's thin smile as he caught the hesitation.

"Apaches did it. More than a dozen of them."

"Apaches?" Braswell snorted. "That's crazy."

"We know there are Apaches scattered through the Sierra del Pino," Ordoñez said, "but they are beaten. They may steal, but they don't kill."

"These do."

Braswell and the captain exchanged doubtful glances. Faver came to his feet, letting his anger show.

"Look, I've scouted for the United States Army. I know Apache sign when I see it. I don't know what's going on here, but if you don't believe me, take a patrol out there and I'll show you."

Ordoñez gazed at him, rubbing his chin thoughtfully. Faver suddenly realized that the young officer wasn't quite as self-assured as he appeared to be. At least, he seemed uncertain how to handle Faver's story.

"Yes," he said finally. "Perhaps Zamora wishes to lure a patrol into an ambush. He might send in a *gringo* deserter with such a tale."

If he expected to draw a heated response, he was disappointed. Faver straightened and folded his arms, his face wooden.

"You have a funny way of showing your gratitude, Captain. If you don't need me anymore, I'd like to get on about my business."

"And what is your business, exactly?"

"Nothing that involves you."

"No?" Ordoñez shrugged. "No matter." He looked at Braswell. "You know something of Zamora's habits—from your customers, of course. What do you think?"

"I don't know." The trader frowned, then thought better of it and leaned back easily in his chair. "Your implications don't bother me, Captain. But this doesn't sound like Zamora."

"No, it doesn't." Ordoñez thought for a moment. "Well, clearly we must send a patrol."

He rose and crossed to an inner door.

"Sergeant!"

"*Sí, Capitán.*"

The door swung back and Faver turned to look at the new arrival. At first glance, he thought the sergeant was the ugliest man he'd ever seen. He was short and squat, but his long arms showed six inches of bare skin at the cuffs of his uniform blouse. His square Indian face was pitted by smallpox, and some old accident or wound had flattened his nose into a shapeless blob. He stood at ease while the captain issued orders to ready a ten-man patrol. Then he glanced at Faver and asked a question that was answered in a language other than Spanish.

The sergeant saluted and left. Ordoñez stood silently a moment, his back to Faver and Braswell.

"My horse was pretty well played out," Faver said at last. "Maybe I could borrow one, if you want me to guide you back."

Without turning, Ordoñez shook his head. "No. Sergeant Noh will serve as our scout. He is very able." He came back to his desk and sat down. "But there are a great many more questions I'd like to ask you, after we have proved you are telling the truth. I hope you'll wait here to answer them when I return with the patrol."

"Sorry."

Faver took a step backward, keeping both Braswell and the captain in sight. He had a sudden feeling of danger, and the dark walls of the office seemed to be closing in on him.

"I was just passing through. I'd rather not stay around."

Ordoñez sighed. There was a strange expression, almost of sadness, on his face. He rapped twice on the desk top with his knuckles, and the sergeant came back in, followed by two soldiers in brown uniforms. Both held rifles trained on Faver.

"I'm afraid," Ordoñez said gently, "I must insist."

CHAPTER 7

Faver had been in jail before. He'd seen the inside of the Tucson and Globe lockups, the first for an argument with a mule skinner holding a low opinion of the cavalry, and the second for a party that got a bit too enthusiastic. He and Nantahe had shared a night or two in the Fort Apache guardhouse, as well, for various offenses against order and discipline. None of those places compared with the dark, narrow cell at the far end of the Guardia barracks.

Barely eight feet square, windowless, with no light except what came through the barred door, the cell closed on Faver like a trap. There were no furnishings, not even a cot, but the packed earthen floor was surprisingly clean. Ordoñez had allowed Faver's blanket roll inside. The saddlebags were still out in the office, beyond the young Guardia private on duty outside the cell.

"You can't arrest this man," Braswell had protested when Ordoñez disarmed Faver and motioned him toward the cells. "You have no reason to believe he's done anything wrong."

"I have no reason to think he hasn't," the captain pointed out. "He is a foreigner who will not explain his presence. Still, he's not under arrest. I merely wish him to remain available until I can verify his story."

"Then what?"

Ordoñez smiled. "*¿Quién sabe?* I'll know more after I've seen the Alvarado *rancho*. Now I must go." His smile vanished and he looked at Faver. "Also, I must talk to Estella. It will be hard for her, if your story is true."

"I'm sorry."

It was the first time Faver had spoken since the sergeant and his men had returned, and Ordoñez looked at him in surprise.

"Yes. Yes, I believe you are." He frowned at Faver a moment

longer, then turned abruptly away. "*Sargento,* come with me. Private Hernandez, see to the prisoner."

That had been a good six hours ago. Hernandez had stood guard at first, then had been relieved—probably to go to supper, Faver thought grimly—by another *soldado*. Aside from that, absolutely nothing had happened.

For the first couple of hours, Faver hardly noticed. He had welcomed the opportunity to think, to sort things out. Braswell, Ordoñez, and Zamora—whoever he was—seemed linked together in a way he couldn't quite understand. Braswell had objected to his arrest, though Faver couldn't see why. He suspected the trader had a good reason for anything he did.

But the real key to the situation was Ordoñez. There was no telling how the young captain would react to what he would find at the raided ranch. He might decide to deport Faver back to the States, or to buck him on to the next highest authority, or even to hold him in jail and hope things would be clearer *mañana*—but it was unlikely he'd hand back Faver's guns and send him on his way without another word. The hunt for Nantahe might end right here.

Another line of thought, less welcome, opened out from there. Nantahe had given his word; the word had been broken and a man was dead. That was simple enough, calling for retribution under both white and Apache law, so Faver had set out to bring Nantahe back.

The killing of Chan-desi had changed things. After that, he knew that Nantahe would never give up, would fight—the old, endless chain, a life for a life—until he was killed.

Now the attack on the Alvarado place had changed the game again. What had started as a duel between Faver and Nantahe was spreading, bringing pain and death to people he had never seen. He could not feel he had done wrong in helping Nantahe to escape, but he couldn't dodge the knowledge that his action had led to all the rest.

For the tenth time, Faver rose from his place against the wall, tried to pace, found the cell was too small. He stepped to the door and glared through the bars at the sentry.

"Don't you people feed prisoners? The captain won't like it if I starve. He has something a lot more interesting planned."

The private jumped, tightened his grip on his rifle. Clearly, he considered Faver a tough customer.

"Did Captain Ordoñez take out the patrol? Is he expected back tonight?"

The soldier stared at him with dark, suspicious eyes and didn't answer.

"Listen, you—"

Faver let his voice trail off. He stood motionless, hands locked on the rusted iron bars. Far back in his mind, he could hear Nantahe laughing at him.

Impatience, worry, helpless anger—those were not Apache traits. A warrior should endure his captivity, taking refuge in silence, denying his feelings, waiting for the moment when his turn would come. That was what Nantahe had done.

Slowly, Faver relaxed his hold on the bars, letting his hands fall loosely to his sides. He turned his back on the doorway and the guard, smoothed out the rumpled bedroll. He had seen hungry camps and hard beds before, and he'd had plenty of practice shutting out thoughts he couldn't afford.

He rolled himself in his blankets and slept.

Morning brought the sound of voices, shouted orders, the familiar clatter of gear and weapons. The guard left and another took his place. A powerful odor of cooking food reminded Faver just how long it had been since his last meal. He lay quietly, listening. There was a lot of activity, even for a military post beginning its day. He wasn't really surprised, a little later, when the door from the captain's office opened and Ordoñez came through.

"You can go," he told the sentry. He came to the door of the cell and looked at Faver. "It was all just as you said. The *rancho*. Everything."

Faver sat up, hugging his knees to his chest. "Figured it would be. Am I still under arrest?"

Ordoñez might not have heard. His thin face was haggard and unshaven, but there was more to it than that. He looked sick, sick and not nearly so tough as the day before.

"We followed the trail of the raiders. There was an arroyo not far from the house. We found Ramón Alvarado there, and his eldest son, and their hired man. They had been—had been—"

"Killed," Faver finished roughly.

"Killed." The captain shook his head. "I have seen death in battle. But this—the things that were done—"

He seemed unable to finish, and Faver didn't help him. The captain had just gotten his first lesson in Apache warfare. Nothing anyone could say would change that.

After a moment's silence, Ordoñez took down a ring of keys. He unlocked the cell and swung the door open.

"This way."

Faver hesitated, remembering suddenly the *ley fuga,* the law of flight, supposedly used by the Mexican rural police to get rid of unwanted prisoners. He had no wish to be shot while trying to escape.

The captain saw his reluctance and flashed white teeth in a quick, grim smile.

"My quarters are down the hall. Perhaps you would like some breakfast and a chance to clean up?"

Faver rubbed a hand over his bristling cheeks and grinned. Slowly, he got to his feet.

"Yeah, I guess I would. Thanks."

Breakfast was a Spartan meal of eggs and tortillas, served by a silent orderly. To Faver, clean and shaved for the first time in days, it was a welcome change from his trail rations. Ordoñez ate little, but drank several cups of the strong, sweet coffee the orderly poured from a silver pot.

"I'm sorry," the captain said suddenly. "A soldier shouldn't mind such things."

Faver shrugged. "I felt the same way." He sipped his coffee. "You haven't been in this part of the country long, I guess."

"Two years, almost. Before, I served in the Yucatán, during the rebellion there."

"And the Army rewarded you by sending you here?"

The captain's eyes narrowed momentarily. Then he smiled, still with a touch of grimness.

"Perhaps. But La Morita is not so bad. The district is quiet, except for Zamora."

"You mentioned Zamora before, back when you didn't believe

me." He paused for a second, but Ordoñez showed no reaction. "Who is he?"

"A bandit." Again, the quick smile. "Or a noble revolutionary, perhaps. It depends on your viewpoint."

He broke off as the orderly came in to clear the table. The man left the coffeepot, stacked dishes and silver on a tray. He came to attention smartly and Ordoñez waved him away.

"That will be all. Another cup, Señor Faver?"

He waited until the door closed behind the orderly, then went on briskly, "Zamora's men raid the mines to the east, steal cattle from the big *haciendas* south of here. This is their home ground. There are many places to hide back in the hills, and the bandits have friends among the people of the *barrancas*."

Faver nodded, remembering the tracks he had cut, the trail that looked as though a troop of cavalry had passed. A couple of things made better sense now.

"I'll bet. That storekeeper—Braswell, his name was?—he wouldn't be one of the friends, would he?"

Ordoñez sat back in his chair. "Señor Braswell is an important man," he said carefully. "He has his own friends, high in the government. Also, he has a great deal of money."

That figured. The bandits would have gold, stolen stock, all kinds of things to sell. They'd need guns and ammunition. There could be a lot of money for a man with connections on both sides of the border. And if the man happened to run a store, he'd have a ready-made cover.

The captain rose, crossed to a low table by the door.

"Cigar? No?" He took one and turned it in his fingers. "My *tropa* has clashed with Zamora—mostly by accident, I'm afraid. Only a couple of my men are regulars. The rest are *Guardia Nacional*—local men. Half are related to Zamora's people. Some spy for him."

"Oh." Faver grinned. "Doesn't sound like you have much chance of catching him."

"I'll get him," Ordoñez said softly. "Someday." Then he looked at Faver. "And now there are the Apaches."

Faver had been waiting for that. The breakfast, the chat with Ordoñez, had all been pleasant enough, but he'd had an idea the captain wasn't quite through asking questions.

Ordoñez didn't look as if he were laying some clever trap. He looked tired and puzzled, not quite sure how to proceed.

"*Señor,* I will speak frankly," he said at last. "I believe your story of the attack on the ranch. But I do not believe in coincidence. For years, *bronco* Apaches have lived in the hills to the south. Except for a few thieves, they make no trouble."

He paused. He was back on balance now, and his eyes were steady on Faver's face.

"Then you appear, and the Alvarado family is murdered. There is a connection there. I must know what it is."

Faver drew a deep breath. There was no way around it. He'd known right along there wouldn't be.

"I'm following two men—Apache scouts, called Nantahe and Chicuelo. They broke loose from a prison train last week and came this way. I think they hooked up with a band of your *broncos* out on a pony raid, and talked them into something bigger."

"But why would they attack the Alvarados? There could be no reason to single them out."

"They weren't singled out," Faver said. "They were just the first ones the Apaches came to. And it won't end there."

Slowly, Ordoñez came back to the table. He pulled back his chair and sat down, then rubbed both hands hard across his face.

"I see," he said at last.

Faver said nothing and, after a moment, the captain raised his head.

"And you? Why are you here?"

"I'm going to take them back. Nantahe, anyway. Back to prison."

Ordoñez raised his eyebrows at the grim intensity in Faver's voice.

"You must hate him very much."

"It's a debt."

Again, Ordoñez let a minute crawl past in silence.

"There's more than your debt, now," he said. "I'll need time to decide. It's my problem, handling the Apaches—and you."

Faver rose slowly, catlike.

"And you figure to keep me locked up while you decide?"

"I'm afraid so."

Faver's eyes moved to the captain's holstered service pistol, measured the distance. Ordoñez smiled.

"Oh, you can escape. You'll probably even make it out of town alive. But you'll have my troops, the Apaches, even Zamora's *bandidos* against you. It would be better to wait."

"Maybe." Faver let his tense muscles uncoil. Wait. Take refuge in silence and hide feeling. Wait. *"Bueno,* Captain. I'll go back to my room now."

He let Ordoñez take him back and close the barred door behind him. There was no guard this time. The captain lingered, looking through the bars.

"One thing I didn't tell you, *señor.* There was another child at the ranch, the nephew of Ramón Alvarado." He closed his eyes for a moment, shook his head as though to throw off a memory. "We didn't find him with the others."

Faver remembered with sudden clarity the print of a small, bare foot in the dust.

"Alvarado's nephew? Then he'd be the brother of that girl— Estella?"

"Señorita Alvarado," the captain corrected. "Yes, he is her brother." He hesitated a moment, then added, "Señorita Alvarado has agreed to become my wife."

Faver thought about that, decided to leave it alone.

"The boy. How old was—is—he?"

"About ten years." Ordoñez touched the bars. "Maybe I ask too much of you. And probably he is dead by now."

Faver gestured impatiently. "Maybe. You can't tell." He rubbed the back of his neck, trying to think. The questions never changed. Where were the hostiles? What would they do next? How did they feel, what did they think? Some of the answers were easy, most weren't—but a scout was supposed to know them all.

"Sometimes Apaches keep captured children as slaves, or even adopt them. It's a custom."

If this bunch of cut-offs still followed the customs. If they had food and space for another child. If it hadn't struck them funny to dump the boy naked in the desert. If anything—but Nantahe was one of this band, and Faver had known him, once.

"I think he's probably alive. He's young enough to be taken into a clan."

The captain's studied composure broke. He swore savagely, slammed a hand against the bars so hard that Faver winced in sympathy. Ordoñez didn't notice the pain.

"I can't even find where they hide! What will Estella feel, thinking Paco alive with those murderers! Better that he were dead!"

Faver closed his eyes, and for a moment was back in the bedroom at the Alvarado place, looking down at the woman who had been Estella's aunt. He shivered, looked at Ordoñez.

"If you believe that, *amigo,*" he said softly, "you haven't learned as much as I thought."

"You cut too many corners, Faver. You and Nantahe think you can make your own rules. You'll pay for that, one day."

The words rang ironically in Faver's memory as he sat hunched in his tiny cell. Randall—Major Gregory Boyd Randall, 10th Cavalry—had told him that more than once during the good years, when Crook commanded the Department of Arizona. Then, it hadn't seemed to matter. Nantahe and Faver were the best, the pick of the scouts, as even Randall reluctantly admitted.

By now, Randall was probably delivering his prisoners in Florida, drawing a reprimand because three had escaped—but if the stocky major could have seen Faver locked snugly in a Mexican jail, he might have smiled to see his prediction fulfilled.

Two days had passed since Faver's talk with the captain. He was more loosely guarded now, allowed food and exercise, but he was still a prisoner. He hadn't seen Ordoñez again, and he was beginning to think he should have tried an escape when he had the chance.

He was sitting on his blanket roll, staring moodily at the opposite wall, when the door from the office opened. Ordoñez rattled keys, then unlocked the cell with a swift, angry motion.

"Come. You have visitors. My office."

Faver blinked at him in surprise, but scrambled up.

"What—?"

"I do this much against my good judgment. Come on."

Not knowing what to expect, Faver preceded him into the office. Two people were waiting there. The trader, Braswell, leaned against the wall, smoking a cigar. He raised his eyebrows in greeting, but before he could speak, Estella Alvarado was in front of Faver, claiming his attention.

"Luis—Capitán Ordoñez—says you think Paco is alive. How do you know?"

Faver took a moment deciding how to answer. He hadn't had much of a chance to look at the girl that day on the square, what with Ordoñez and the baby to worry about. She looked eighteen or nineteen, taller than he'd remembered, with a leggy, coltish awkwardness. She'd have been pretty without the lines of grief etched around her mouth, the redness in her dark eyes.

"I don't know that he's alive. It seems likely, though." He saw hope dawn in her face, quickly put out a hand. "Now, wait. There's no way to be sure."

"But now the soldiers can find him and bring him back." She clapped her hands together, turned to Ordoñez. "Now you must find the Apaches."

Reluctantly, his eyes on Faver, the captain shook his head.

"They will have a *ranchería* somewhere, hidden, well defended. They would be waiting for us in ambush, or they would escape by another way."

"Are you afraid, then? Perhaps you don't wish to fight."

Ordoñez shrugged, still avoiding her eyes. He jerked his head at Faver. "Tell her."

"He's right," Faver said. "Troops could never surprise them. Even if they did, the Apaches would never let Paco be captured alive. They'd kill him first."

The girl stood very still, her head bowed. Faver saw her shoulders slump, saw the light go out of her eyes.

"You are saying there's nothing you can do. Nothing."

Braswell snorted and pulled himself erect. He glared at Faver and Ordoñez, but when he spoke, his voice was soft. "I told you, 'Stella. They're right. Come on, I'll take you home."

Blindly, she turned toward him. Faver moved suddenly, caught her arm. Here was his way out of the cell. It might not be the best way, but he didn't have time to be particular.

"I can do it. I can get the boy back."

They stared at him, blank surprise on the girl's face, disbelief on Braswell's. Across the room, Ordoñez made a strangled sound of protest, but Faver ignored him.

"If Paco's alive, I'll find him. I know Apaches, and I know Nantahe."

Braswell laughed. "Just you, all by yourself? Are you going to sneak up on the Apaches?"

"That's right," Faver said. "Any objections?"

For a moment, Braswell seemed to weigh the challenge in Faver's eyes. Then he laughed nervously and turned to Ordoñez.

"This *hombre* talks mighty big from the jail. Maybe if you let him out, you'll never see him again."

The captain didn't answer directly, and Faver almost laughed. Probably Ordoñez wouldn't consider it much of a disaster if he never came back.

"There are many Apaches in the *barrancas*," Ordoñez said at last. "Most are peaceful. If you move against the wrong ones—"

"I can tell Apaches apart," Faver snapped. "Can you?"

He might have said more, but Estella broke in. She had shaken herself free of her momentary trance, and now looked eagerly at him.

"Señor Faver—Jess." She stumbled over the name. "You'd do this?" Before he could answer, she rushed on. "You saved Paquito at the ranch, where he would have died, and we—I—accused you of terrible things. Even now, I haven't thanked you."

"*De nada,*" Faver said, hiding his shame at the way he was using her, as he'd hidden his other emotions. "You were scared."

"No, it's not nothing." She caught his hands impulsively. Her wide, dark eyes held a depth of gratitude he knew he didn't deserve. "It's wonderful. And now you would risk your life for Paco."

"Not for Paco," Faver said, looking into her face. She lowered her head and hurriedly regained her hands. There was a trace of pink in her cheeks. She'd taken it as Faver had intended, though not exactly as he'd meant it. Now he looked at Ordoñez.

"How about it, *Capitán?*"

The Mexican's face was impassive, but the set of his jaw didn't bode any special good for Faver. He clearly hadn't liked that conversation.

"It is most irregular."

"Luis," the girl said. "Think of Paco."

"I *am* thinking of him," Ordoñez said grimly, "but I'm also thinking of the district. My *tropa* is spread thin on patrols. If there is a full-scale war, we'll have many children like Paco."

Faver rubbed the back of his neck. "Seems to me you've got your war, Captain." He paused, then spoke straight to Ordoñez. "There won't be any peace, as long as Nantahe and Chicuelo are alive."

"Yes." Ordoñez nodded slowly. "As long as they are alive."

Braswell had been watching blankly. Now he suddenly shook himself and interrupted.

"Captain?" Ordoñez turned politely. "Captain, I think Faver's crazy, and looking to get killed. But if he's determined to go, I'll stake him to supplies." He shrugged, looked embarrassed. "Hell, it's worth a try."

Faver looked at him in astonishment, then grinned. Maybe the trader was serious, or maybe he also thought this was a good way to get rid of a potential nuisance. His help was welcome, whatever its motive.

"Luis," Estella said. "Luis, in the name of God!"

Ordoñez might have been convinced anyway, but he would have been less than human if he could have withstood the naked plea in the girl's voice. Abruptly, he nodded.

"It is settled, then. When do you want to start?"

"Soon. Tomorrow, if I can be ready by then."

"Thank you, *señor*." Estella Alvarado took his hand again. This time, her dark eyes held no trace of the confusion she'd shown earlier. Bowing her head over the hand, she pressed it to her lips. "May all the saints go with you."

For a moment, Faver felt a renewed stab of guilt, but only for a moment. He had to get free, by whatever means. He'd try to find the boy, but that wasn't the most important thing. What had begun as a warrior's debt had slipped far out of his control. He had to find Nantahe and end it while he could.

CHAPTER 8

Braswell's store was cool and dark inside. There were no windows, but slanting bars of sunlight squeezed through the open spaces below the eaves. The light fell in bright patches on the floor, making the shadows below the high rafters seem even deeper.

"I brought those rafters in from Marathon," Braswell said. "No timber around here. The floorboards, too. This is the only building in La Morita with a wooden floor."

"You must do a good business," Faver said. He wasn't really interested. His mind was on the business ahead. At least, it should have been, but he found his thoughts had an annoying way of coming back to the Alvarado girl. He'd halfway expected her to be here.

"Business is fair. Barter, mostly." Braswell kicked at a bundle on the floor. "There's my big money-maker."

Faver knelt to look and saw a mass of leafless, gray-green plants.

"Candelilla," the trader said. "We render it down for wax. They use it for waterproofing, in the States."

"You grow it here?"

Braswell shrugged. "It grows itself. The *peones* gather it back in the hills. I send a wagon around to pick it up every month."

"Oh?" Faver sat back on his heels, looking up innocently. "I'm surprised Zamora's bandits don't bother you."

The trader's face hardened into a scowl. When he spoke, his voice had lost its gossipy tone.

"Maybe it's because I mind my own business."

"Maybe." That was enough, Faver thought. He knew where Braswell stood, but it wasn't his problem. "Do you have the things I asked for?"

Braswell jerked his head toward the back of the building. "In the storeroom. Food and ammunition and all the rest. Figured you'd want to pack it yourself."

"That's right. How about horses?"

"Well, I have a good saddle horse for you, and the gray will do for a pack animal." Braswell stroked his beard thoughtfully. "That buckskin of yours is a fine mount. Sure you want to leave him?"

"Keep him for me. Unshod ponies are better where I'm going."

Braswell shrugged. "Well, I don't want to tell you your trade. Is there anything else you need?"

Coming easily to his feet, Faver looked around the big room. There were shelves with hardware and a few canned goods, bolts of brightly colored cloth, sacks of sugar and rice and coffee piled against the far wall. The roofbeams were hung with pelts of coyote and bobcat, with strings of gourds and bright red chilies.

"I was looking for a present," Faver said. "I guess I'll need a goat."

He rode into the canyon openly this time. He knew he'd been watched off and on almost from the moment he'd left town, but it didn't matter. He didn't need to cover his tracks until he knew where he was going.

The old woman, Juana, was sitting by the doorway to her hut. A ragged blanket was drawn around her shoulders and she seemed to be asleep. Faver drew rein and looped the lead rope of his packhorse around the saddle horn. The goat he carried across his saddlebow bleated plaintively. Juana opened her eyes at the sound.

"Hello, Grandmother," Faver said. "I'm still alive."

"For today." Juana sighed. "Don't sit there like an owl in a tree. Get down."

Faver swung to the ground, setting the goat down on its spindly legs. It bleated and ran off toward the pen where the others were kept. Juana cackled with laughter.

"And bringing a present, too. If I was twenty years younger, I'd think you were courting."

"If you were twenty years younger, I would be," he said, "but not with one goat. I'll bet you were a twenty-horse woman."

The old woman put a hand over her mouth and giggled. "For

you, one goat might have been enough. If your hands are as quick as your tongue, you must be a terror with the night-crawlers on the reservation."

Faver grinned. "You never night-crawled, did you, Grandmother? You were a respectable girl."

"Respectable enough not to get caught." She ran her hands across her cheeks and down over her withered breasts. "Well, I'm respectable now, and no mistake. And you aren't here because you like old women. What do you want?"

"Nantahe."

"I told you. I've got no reason to help you. All you bring is trouble."

Faver stiffened suddenly, scanning the willows upstream along the creek. He saw nothing, but he was sure there'd been a movement there a moment before. Juana's eyes flicked that way, came quickly back to Faver.

"Trouble, Grandmother?" He dropped to one knee in front of her, speaking softly. "You know what real trouble means. You've seen the children hungry and the young men killed. Do you want that to happen again, here?"

Juana's voice was harsh. "I want to be left alone. Why do you come to me?"

"The cut-offs are getting stronger. They have a boy, Paco Alvarado. I'm going to get him back. Then I'm going to get Nantahe."

This time there was no mistaking the rustle among the willows, the glimpse of a brown-skinned arm. Faver pivoted on his knee, his hand dropping to the butt of the long-barreled Remington.

"No!" Juana said sharply.

Faver hesitated a moment, looking at her narrowly. Then he seated the pistol in its holster and took his hand away. Juana sighed.

"My grandson. He thinks he's protecting me."

"He's been following me," Faver said. "For Nantahe?"

Juana was silent a moment. Something changed in her face, and she suddenly seemed tired and very old.

"It's true," she murmured, not looking at Faver. "They'll get him into it, him and the others who were too young to fight before. And the soldiers will come."

Faver said nothing. He stood up and caught the reins of his horse.

Juana folded her hands in her lap and bowed her head. She spoke almost in a whisper.

"To the south, there's a long mountain, hollow inside like a drinking gourd. Anybody looking for troublemakers might go there."

"Thanks." Faver swung into the saddle and reined the horse around. "Thank you, Grandmother."

The old woman raised her head. Tears shone in her eyes, but she smiled weakly. "Come again," she said. "Bring another goat."

Faver grinned. "If I find the boy, I'll bring a cow," he promised.

"Be careful, white-eye," Juana called as he rode out. "I could use a cow."

By nightfall, he was deep in the foothills south of the Alvarado place. He'd gotten a map of the area from Ordoñez, and he found Juana's mountain on it without difficulty. The map showed no sign of a hollow, but Faver was sure the old woman had been telling the truth. The hollow was there, and there would be at least two ways into it, for no Apache would let himself be bottled up. All Faver had to do was find the trails. At least, that would do for a start.

He camped in a sheltered canyon, rode south again at dawn. This time, he followed an erratic course and doubled back often to watch his backtrail. He made an early camp at a small spring, satisfied that he was no longer being followed. As he sliced bread and salt pork for his supper, he thought about the renegades' hideout.

"Don't trust your luck," Nantahe had told him once, back when he was learning. "Luck gets you killed. Plan what you do."

It was good advice, but he couldn't do much planning this time. The map showed a canyon winding out of the northern end of the mountains, near the Chihuahua road. That was probably one entrance, and would surely be guarded. High, unbroken cliffs blocked access from the south and west, so the other door had to be somewhere along the east side of the range. The land was more open there, shelving into desert without roads or settlements. That was where the Apaches should be least watchful, and that was where Faver would go.

He fed and watered the horses, checked their unshod hooves carefully for splits or stones. He was up and moving after midnight, holding south by the stars and the set of the ridges, and soon the barren mesas of the desert rose around him. Just before dawn, he cut a fresh trail. Horses, most of them riderless, had passed that way within the last day or two. Their tracks curved back toward the twin peaks of Juana's mountain.

With the first light of dawn, he found a sheltered spot among the boulders at the base of one of the mesas. He picketed the horses there, going out on foot to scout the area. He found other trails, some recent, others months old; all led the same way. Evidently the Apaches felt completely safe behind their stretch of desert. Faver grinned. He'd try to change that.

Watching from the rim of the mesa just at sunset, he saw dust hanging above the low hills a couple of miles away. Cacti and gnarled juniper trees struggled for a foothold there, and a flock of birds was circling in that direction. The birds meant water, and the dust meant somebody to drink it. Faver smiled and slipped back to the horses to wait for dark.

If the Apaches had been more careful, they might have pulled Faver into a trap. As it was, they came close. They had made camp at the foot of a broad, steep-sided mesa. Close against the rock was a tiny pool, fed by pour-off from the mesa top during the infrequent rains. The water was green and slimy, but it was water, and that was enough.

Faver came in on foot, far from the well-worn trail. He saw the glow of a fire in the little hollow by the pool, caught the distant murmur of voices. Silently, Faver flattened himself in a clump of brush, looking for a way to get closer. An instant before he was ready to go on, one of the shadows on the ridgeline moved.

Faver froze. The shadow came closer, became an Apache. He stood for a moment on the crest, the stars of the Hunter sharp behind him. Then he came farther from the firelight, staring out into the darkness. Faver drew his knife, holding his breath as a moccasined foot came down within three yards of him, but the Indian moved on and finally crossed back into the hollow.

Softly as a shadow, Faver followed. Three horses were picketed near the pool, and two more Apaches squatted around a tiny fire. They were drinking something from long-necked bottles, and one of them held out a bottle to the returning sentry.

"Ho, Bonito. Did you find your night-ghosts?"

The first man didn't smile. He jerked his head in a quick negative motion as he lowered himself to the ground.

"I heard something, Scar," he said flatly.

Faver scowled. He could have sworn he hadn't made enough noise to matter, but the overhanging rocks must magnify every sound. He should have known that. Maybe he really was losing his edge.

"Falling rocks, or a coyote," the third Apache said. He glanced toward the mesa. "The walls talk here."

Bonito shrugged. One of the horses whickered, and Faver took advantage of the moment to slip into the shadows below a twisted juniper. He could see the Indians clearly, but they should be blind to anything outside the circle of firelight.

The one called Bonito rose and yanked an old dragoon revolver from his belt. He walked over to the horses, resting his hand on the neck of a rangy pinto while he stood listening.

"Ghosts, again."

That was the second Apache, and this time Faver could see him. He was a lean, stringy man, and his tangled hair hung, unbound, to his shoulders. An old scar furrowed his cheek from temple to lips, lifting the corner of his mouth in a perpetual sneer.

"Who do you think is there, Bonito? The white-eye our leaders are so worried about?"

Faver caught his breath sharply, released it as he realized they didn't know he was there—but it looked as if he'd come to the right place.

"Our leaders!" Bonito mimicked. He came back to his place by the fire, took a long pull from the bottle. "Leading us into trouble! Before they came, we didn't have *soldados* after us."

"Before they came, you hid in the hills," the third Apache said calmly. He seemed to be drinking less than the others, Faver noted. "You didn't complain when you took that gun in the raid."

"Maybe I've thought about it. Those wild men will bring the lancers down on us. I don't mean to die for them."

Scar grinned. "You know, Hos-tay talked the same way. He even offered to fight about it." He paused, enjoying himself. "Chicuelo cut his liver out."

"He doesn't scare me." Bonito took out the pistol and rested it across his knees. "He's only another man, not some mountain spirit. A bullet in the back will kill him."

"Shut up, Bonito!" The third man looked hard at Bonito. "A man smart enough to do that should be smart enough not to talk about it. I'm going to sleep, before I say something Chicuelo will hear."

Scar rose angrily, but the other turned his back and began to spread his blankets near the fire. There was a silence, and then Scar laughed.

"What's wrong with him? Come on, Bonito, help me finish the whiskey."

Bonito suddenly looked much more sober. Hesitantly, he shook his head.

"No—ah—I'm sleepy, too. Should we keep a watch?"

Scar laughed again, but Faver didn't think he sounded amused. "Against what? Ghosts and white-eyes? Go to sleep."

He kicked dirt over the embers of the fire, plunging the scene into sudden darkness. For a moment, Faver was blinded. He knew he should move quickly, before the eyes of the Apaches had time to adjust, but any noise might draw a bullet. Instead, he lay silent while Scar and Bonito rolled themselves in their blankets.

The horses shifted restlessly on the picket line. Down by the pool, a frog began piping. One of the Indians started to snore, broke off with a grunt and a sudden movement. It was far along toward morning, and the sleepers had been quiet for more than an hour, when Faver finally left the hollow and padded away into the night.

He filled his water bags at the pool the next day. The Apaches had pulled out two hours before, heading off toward the long bulk of the mountain. Faver followed cautiously. Before noon, he cut a dim trail that led away toward the south, and he turned that way without hesitation. The land was higher there, sloping up into barren foothills. Faver needed a high place away from the well-traveled routes, where he could watch the comings and goings across the desert and scout his approach to the mountain.

He was lucky, for within a mile his trail turned to parallel what seemed to be the route the Apaches had followed. Sheltered from observation by intervening ridges, the way climbed steadily up from the desert floor. Before long, Faver found water again, a seeping spring among scattered boulders. The water was strongly alkaline, and the tracks around it were few and old. Faver unsaddled the horses and hobbled them to graze. Taking canteen and rifle, he climbed the ridge to his right, looking for a vantage point above the main trail.

It was going well, he thought as he settled into a hollow along the crest. The Apaches were off guard, and he'd had luck. Now he was close to their hideout. He was short of food, but there was plenty around him. Most men wouldn't see it, but he was as much at home here as the renegades, and nobody starved at home.

Dust rose back among the mesas and crawled closer like a woolly caterpillar until Faver could see men and horses at its base. There were two Apaches this time, driving six or seven horses. They passed below Faver, less than a mile away, and were lost to sight on the lower slopes of the mountains. From his spot on the ridge, he could see a crack in the frowning line of cliffs below the tallest peak, a narrow canyon reaching back toward the heart of the range. The riders seemed to be headed there.

No one else passed on the trail until late afternoon. The dust then was not a cloud, but a thin film, whirled away by the rising wind. Between the hills, Faver saw a single rider coming in. The Apache paused and dismounted for a moment, then came on more slowly until he was lost behind the hills.

"One more," Faver muttered, switching his gaze to the point where the Indian would come back into sight. Everybody he'd seen so far had been going in. Maybe Nantahe and Chicuelo were gathering their forces for another raid, or maybe they were drawing in to get clear of the Guardia patrols.

There were other possibilities, but he shrugged the question off. He'd have time enough to worry when he found the village. Maybe he could follow this last Apache in close enough to get a look at the mouth of that canyon.

Minutes dragged by, and the Indian didn't reappear. That was odd. If he'd been planning to stop for the night, he should have camped back by the pour-off pool, but the place where Faver had first seen him was well past the pool, almost—

The realization hit Faver like a cold fist in the belly. He twisted to face the way he'd come, cocking the hammer of his carbine. Viciously, he cursed himself for stupidity—for foolish, blind over-confidence. The Apache had stopped at the point where the trails divided. He'd seen fresh tracks leading toward the alkali spring and had come to investigate. Faver was being stalked.

For a full minute, he crouched motionless, watching his back-trail. The Indian might have gone for help but it wasn't likely. The tracks weren't that suspicious-looking, and no warrior would risk exposing himself to ridicule without checking first.

No, it would be one against one, and to the death. Faver couldn't let the Apache get back to warn the others.

He realized what he was thinking and grinned tightly. Right now, he had a more immediate problem. He had to stay alive long enough to find the warrior.

Carbine ready at his hip, he worked back toward the horses. At first he went in short rushes, holding to cover and moving to flank likely spots for an ambush, but the Apache had been smart enough not to follow Faver's trail up the hillside. He would be watching the spring, waiting for Faver to return. He might not know Faver was aware of him, but that was one chance Faver decided not to take.

Circling wide, he crossed well below the spring and came up on the far side. The wind was blowing now in sharp gusts, sweeping clouds of dust along the face of the ridge. The Apache had set himself with the wind at his back, and that was where Faver found him, crouched in the ragged vee between two boulders.

Faver came in from behind, slowly and silently. He couldn't see the Indian's face, but from the motionless intensity of the coppery back, he knew the man was watching the trail above the spring. His hands held a short bow with an arrow nocked and ready.

Without taking his eyes from the watcher, Faver reached out and leaned the carbine against a rock. He was barely ten yards from his man. If he could cover it in one rush, he could kill the Apache without shooting. He tensed, closing his hand around the haft of his knife.

Then something—sound or feeling or animal sense of danger—warned the Apache. Instantly, he turned like a cat, the bowstring coming smoothly back to his ear. Faver hurled himself aside as the barbed steel arrowhead struck sparks on the rock by his head. Already the warrior was fitting a second arrow to the string.

All thought of silence forgotten, Faver snatched for his pistol, bringing it up as the Indian drew his bow. The echoing crash of the shot seemed enormously loud among the boulders. The Apache lurched backward and fell. His loosed arrow clattered harmlessly behind Faver.

Faver came forward slowly and rolled the Apache over. He was surprised at the slightness of the body. The Indian had been young, not more than seventeen, a skinny kid not yet full-grown. Faver's bullet had caught him squarely in the chest. He was dead. It had started, the killing of the young ones, just as he'd warned Juana it would.

"No gun." Faver shook his head. "If he'd had a gun—"

He left the rest of the thought unspoken. Beside the spring, the horses were pawing nervously, their heads up and their nostrils strained wide. There was no other movement.

The boy had been alone. Unless he was expected at the *ranchería*, it might be days before anyone thought to wonder about him. Meanwhile, Faver could only hope his shot had gone unheard.

He shook his head. There were too many ifs, but he didn't really have any choice. It would never be easier to get in, and he'd come too far to stop—but he would have to hurry.

CHAPTER 9

There were Apaches below, more than a dozen of them. They were women. The oldest was a wrinkled grandmother, the youngest a half-grown girl who would soon be receiving suitors. They laughed and chatted freely as they stooped beneath the pines. They were gathering *piñon* nuts, and they were completely unaware of Jess Faver's presence.

Faver lay on a rocky ledge almost a hundred feet above them, carbine and field glasses by his side. In the two days since he'd killed the Apache at the alkali spring, he'd moved closer to the mountains, climbing the lower slopes at night. The main trail had run through a sheer-walled canyon. Its mouth was guarded, so Faver had left his horses and most of his supplies in a safe place and made his way on foot up and over the crest. The climb was long and dangerous, but he'd made it. He was inside.

Juana had been right about the valley. It did resemble a drinking gourd, broad and deep, scooped from the heart of the mountains. A little stream rose somewhere at the upper end, flowed the valley's full length, and poured out into the canyon where the main trail ran. A second trail, narrow and half overgrown in brush, led north through another canyon toward the La Morita road.

As Faver watched, two Apache warriors came along the nearer bank of the stream. He edged back, but they passed beneath his perch without a glance. They splashed through the shallow water and strode on up the valley, one of them pausing to call a greeting to the women. The young girl straightened to look after them.

"Fill your basket, Pretty-mouth." A heavyset woman sat back on her haunches and leered at her. "Those two will be sniffing around you soon enough."

The one called Pretty-mouth hastily went back to her work, ducking her head as if to hide from the laughter.

"They may do more than sniff," another woman put in loudly. "That young one, anyway. Will your belt still tie, little flower?"

Faver didn't wait to see how the girl reacted to the teasing. He eased back from the rim, seeking a clear path around to his left. The village had to be up that way, near the source of the creek. So far, the guards on the trail and the two renegades who had just passed were the only warriors Faver had seen in the valley. There had been no sign of Nantahe or Chicuelo.

He worked his way across the slope, trying to keep covered both above and below. Moving by daylight was risky, but not as risky as climbing the valley's walls in the dark—and the guards all seemed to be watching for danger from the outside, not for trouble in their hideaway.

He found the *ranchería* on a flat, grassy bench near the spring that fed the stream. There were almost twenty wickiups, some solidly built and covered with hides against the coming winter, others appearing newly thrown together. A herd of horses grazed in a meadow above the village, watched by two young boys. Other children played along the sandy bank of the creek, and Faver brought out the field glasses to watch them.

They were healthy-looking kids, four girls and three boys, kicking at a ball made of deer hide. Faver rested the glasses on the oldest boy for a moment, then shook his head and shifted back to scan the wickiups. The Apaches might be holding the Alvarado boy inside for some reason. Or, of course, they might not have him at all.

In an open space between the huts, two women were tending a cooking pot hung over a bed of coals. They seemed to be deep in conversation, one of them breaking off now and then to stir the simmering stew. Faver's stomach reminded him that he'd been on a diet of salt pork and jerky for long enough. He wondered what was in the pot. It might be rabbit or venison, but it could equally well be mule or dog or field rat seasoned with dried caterpillars. He'd tried them all at one time or another, and he remembered how Nantahe had laughed when he was unable to keep the rat-and-caterpillar mixture down.

One of the women turned toward the nearest wickiup and

called out sharply. When there was no answer, she stooped to the doorway and called again, this time loud enough for Faver to hear. He caught his breath and trained his glasses on the hut.

The boy came out slowly. He didn't look frightened. His eyes were swollen from crying, and there was a purpling bruise across the left side of his face, left over from the raid, Faver guessed—the Apaches didn't beat children. He wore a breechclout and high-topped tegua moccasins. That meant he'd been adopted, not taken as a slave. It might make things easier.

The woman spoke quietly, pointing toward the back of the wickiup. The boy—Paco, Estella had called him—went there and returned with an armload of firewood. When he started to go back inside, the woman shook her head, motioning toward the creek and lower valley. Faver grinned, understanding as clearly as if he could hear her words. Don't sit around inside. Go and play. Get out from underfoot for a while. It was a gesture neither white nor Indian, just human.

Paco went off slowly, swinging well clear of the children playing with the ball. Faver silently thanked the boy's foster mother. If Paco would only wander a little farther from the camp, Faver would have a chance to reach him.

If he wanted to. That thought cropped up even as he looked for a quick way down from the rim. Any plan of escape would involve talking to the boy, then waiting for nightfall. It would be a big risk —a long time to trust a ten-year-old child—and Paco was safe enough where he was.

There was another thing. Faver hadn't seen more than half a dozen men, even counting the three guards at the pass. The others, the ones he'd seen crossing the desert, must have ridden out while he was making his climb. He could find a good place, hole up and wait for Nantahe and Chicuelo to return. Then it would be two hundred yards and downhill from the rim, a clean shot for the Springfield and a good chance of getting away afterward. If he tried to rescue Paco, the chance might never come again. The renegades would never be careless enough to let him find them a second time.

Paco was out of sight along the creek bank now, and still Faver didn't move. Finally, he shook his head. Ordoñez wouldn't approve, but he wasn't ready to shoot Nantahe from ambush. If it

came to killing, it would be face-to-face, with both of them knowing why. Meanwhile, there was the boy.

He didn't take time to consider how much Estella Alvarado's
soft voice and the pressure of her hand on his own had to do with
his decision. He merely snapped the Springfield into its sling and
began a cautious descent into the valley.

It took more than an hour to get safely into cover among the
trees and almost another hour to find Paco. The boy had wandered far from the creek, to the tumbled rocks scattered at the
base of the valley's steep western wall. Alternately crawling and
sprinting, feeling completely naked in the open, Faver reached a
tangle of brush thirty yards away. He lay still for a minute, letting
breathing and heartbeat slow to normal, confirming that he still
hadn't been seen. Then he moved again.

Paco was sitting on a boulder, his arms wrapped around his
knees, his head bowed. He heard a soft rustle behind him and
turned, opening his mouth to cry out. Then a strong hand clamped
off his shout and dragged him backward and down into the lee of
the boulder.

"Quiet." Faver realized he'd spoken in Apache and switched to
Spanish. *"No tengas miedo.* Don't be afraid. I come from Estella
to help you."

At first, the boy didn't seem to understand. He kicked and
fought; his teeth found a grip on Faver's hand and clamped down.
Only when Faver repeated Estella's name did his struggles weaken.
At last, he relaxed, looking up into Faver's face with mounting comprehension.

Slowly, Faver eased his hand from the boy's mouth. Paco drew
a deep breath and Faver tensed, but it came out in a silent, racking sob. Faver awkwardly stroked the tangled black hair while
Paco buried his face against him and cried.

He let it go on as long as he could, but there wasn't much time.
Abruptly, he held the boy away and shook him by his skinny
shoulders.

"You have to get back up on that rock. Somebody might notice
that you're gone. Don't make any noise. Don't talk unless I tell
you, just sit and listen. Can you do that?"

Paco tried to speak, but he couldn't get anything out at first. He
gulped and began to knuckle the tears from his eyes.

"I—I think so."

"*Bueno*. Good boy. Go."

Faver gave him a boost, and he clambered back to his place on the boulder. He must have wanted to ask about Faver, to pour out the story of the raid, to show some emotion at finding a friend from outside, but he had learned from his captors. He sat very still, his face blank. That was good, Faver thought, very good. They might get out of this after all.

"Look back toward the camp," Faver whispered. "Not at me. We're leaving tonight, going back to Estella. *¿Comprende?*"

Paco nodded. Faver rubbed at his hand. It was bleeding where the boy had bitten him, and that somehow pleased him.

"That hut you came out of. Are they keeping you there?"

Another nod.

"Who stays there? Do they tie you at night?"

"No, I am not tied." Paco's voice was louder than Faver would have liked, but it was steady and under control. "Magdalena and another lady, her sister, live there. They don't have any boys or girls—that's why they wanted me. And Delgadito stays there, but he went away with the other men last night."

"Good. You have to stay awake tonight until everyone else is asleep."

"All right."

"As soon as the moon goes behind that mountain, come outside. I'll be waiting by the stream."

"But what if somebody wakes up? What if they see me?"

"Don't say anything. Just wait, and pretend to go to sleep. I'll come after you. All right?"

"I'm afraid," the boy said simply. Then Faver saw his back stiffen. "Somebody comes!"

Faver's hand went to his knife. Here was the first test. One wrong word, one careless glance by Paco, and Faver would have to fight his way out—if he could. His life, both their lives, rested on Paco's frail shoulders.

"*¡Cabrón!* Mexican coward!"

It was a child's voice. Sand and grit from the boulder trickled down on Faver as Paco got to his feet. The voice was joined by others, laughing, taunting the boy. Young Apaches, like most children, could be hard on newcomers, and Paco must have been easy game for them at first.

"You don't scare me!" Paco's yell startled Faver. The boy leaped down on the far side of the rock. "Come and fight!"

There were more yells and the sounds of a scuffle, which slowly moved away. Paco seemed to be trying to lead the others back toward the village. Then a woman's voice cut in over the high-pitched cries of the children.

"Troublemakers. *Bandidos.* Go on, scat!"

Faver heard a splash and strangled an urge to laugh. He'd seen Apache women break up fights before. A big pot of cold water did wonders to calm down young combatants.

"Behave like dogs, get treated like dogs," the woman sniffed. "Come along, Paco. I told you not to make trouble."

"Sí, Magdalena. I'm sorry," the boy said meekly.

Faver lay still until there were no more sounds nearby, then peered around the boulder. The woman was leading Paco back toward the camp. The other children, their fight forgotten, had already gone back to their game along the creek. Faver relaxed his grip on his knife and leaned back in relief against the rock. Only then did he realize that his shirt was soaked with sweat.

The moon had been down for almost half an hour. Faver lay in the tall grass along the creek and worried. If the boy had been caught, it could be bad. There was no telling what he might say, what kind of a trap might be waiting. Or maybe he had only fallen asleep.

An inch at a time, Faver raised his head to look over the sandy cutbank. He had smeared his face with dirt—not that much additional smearing had been needed—so he would be almost invisible in the deep shadows.

Nothing moved in or around the village. Higher up, he could just make out the dark blur of the pony herd. As he'd expected, the horses had been rounded up at dusk and brought into a stone corral near the huts. There were no guards, but the village held three or four men, at least—and, as Juana had said, even an old woman could pull a trigger.

Faver sighed. His plan, such as it was, was weak enough without his going in after Paco, dodging dogs and Lord knew what

else, but time was passing, and he'd promised to come. Wishing he
had a squadron of cavalry at his back, he wriggled over the bank
and elbowed his way toward the wickiup.

He'd barely gone ten yards when something moved off to his
left. He had expected it and he was ready. He rolled to one side,
swinging the carbine up and into line, hammer back, his finger
closing on the trigger.

"*¡Yo—señor!*"

Paco was a small, dark figure against the sky. Shakily, Faver
lowered the carbine's hammer to half-cock. He grabbed the boy,
yanking him down into the shelter of the bank, but it was too late.
His cry had been loud enough to carry. A dog barked in the village and others joined in. A woman's voice called out sleepily.

"It was so long," Paco whispered. He was trying not to cry.
"Magdalena stayed awake so late, and then I—I went to sleep."

"It's all right." Faver patted the boy's head absently. They had
to hurry. There was no time for plans now, no time to go over the
ridge, no time for anything. There was only one chance, and if it
failed, there was nothing. "Paco, come on. We have to run."

He hauled Paco up and half-dragged him along the gentle slope
toward the corral. This bunch was careless, as Apaches went, but
surely they weren't stupid. There had to be a horse or two bridled
and ready in case of trouble in the night. At least, Faver hoped so.

Twenty yards to go. He kept his eyes on the ground, trying to
pick sure footing in the darkness, but his mind was concentrating
on the noise from the camp. Fifteen yards—a stumble, recovery.
The single voice had grown to a confused babble, questions and
sleepy protests. Ten yards, five. Then he was vaulting the low wall
while horses shied away, reaching back to pull Paco over.

A pole gate blocked the entrance to the corral. Beside the gate,
a horse was tied, bridled and with a blanket on its back.

"Only one," Faver muttered. "Paco, get up."

He swung Paco up onto the animal's back and passed him the
reins. The boy shifted, sitting the horse well and holding the reins
like he knew how to handle them. He'd better, Faver thought.

"You know the trail to the north? The one up away from the
creek?"

Paco nodded. He looked wide-eyed toward the wickiups, then

back at Faver. The horses were moving restlessly, snorting and pawing, making a commotion the Apaches could surely hear.

"Go out that way. Ride slow and keep to the shadows. You'll come out close to the road. Go until you find help. Understand?"

"But—there are guards."

Faver was already sliding back the gate. "There won't be. Go!"

Someone was coming up from the camp. Above the other voices, a man's shout rose suddenly.

"Who's that? Chato, look to the horses!"

Faver pivoted, snatching up the Springfield and firing from the hip. The carbine's roar and muzzle flash seemed enormous in the darkness. The heavy slug slammed into something—a log, he thought—among the wickiups. A woman screamed, and the moving figures scattered.

"C Troop! By the right flank, wheel!" Faver bellowed. He gave Paco's pony a slap on the rump and it clattered away, the boy clinging desperately to the reins. The other horses were rearing and plunging, already beginning to pour out the open gate. Faver grabbed a handful of mane as one went past, dragged himself up. He got one leg over and hung on, riding low on the animal's off side, his free hand clawing for his pistol.

"K Troop, at the gallop! Charge!"

It wasn't much of a performance, in his opinion, but the Indians were confused by the darkness and the galloping hooves, shocked by the invasion of their fortress. Faver fired three shots into the air, yelling madly, and the spooked horses swung out of the corral and tore off down the valley.

Shots came from the village, scattered and inaccurate. A pony off to Faver's right screamed and went down, carrying another with it in a tangle of flailing hooves. Faver gave up his shouting and merely hung on, hoping his new mount wouldn't stumble. He'd made enough noise to attract everyone in the place. It might not be enough to give Paco cover, but it would have to do.

When the first rush of the horses slowed, Faver clamped down with his knees and began to work toward the edge of the herd. The pony responded beautifully, and Faver urged him on. The stampede had taken them well into the canyon that led down to the desert floor. It was dangerous to take that way out, but noth-

ing was as dangerous as staying where he was. He pulled up
briefly to reload pistol and carbine, then rode on.

A half-mile from the canyon's mouth, he eased the pony back
into a walk. Dawn was breaking, touching the cliffs with vivid orange. The canyon floor was still deep in shadow, but an alert sentry might see sudden movement, and the drum of hoofbeats carried a long way.

The decision probably saved his life. Before he reached the next
turn in the trail, he heard the sound of many horses coming up the
canyon. He pulled up sharply just as a pair of mounted Apaches
rounded the boulders less than fifty yards ahead.

Faver's hand whipped to his holster and brought up the old
Remington. The Indians stared at him, their impassivity giving
way for once to blank astonishment. Then one recovered and
raised his rifle.

"¡Ai, hombre! ¿Quién es?"

Faver fired, ripping off six shots as fast as he could thumb the
hammer. There was no hope of hitting anything in the shifting
light, but he might discourage them for a moment. The two might
be sentries hurrying to the ranchería, or the point for the main
body returning from a raid. Either way, he had to shake them
quickly.

Bending low over the pony's neck, he pounded back the way he
had come. Rifles cracked behind him and a chorus of angry shouts
showed that others had joined the chase. He was headed back toward the ranchería now, and the aroused warriors there would already be looking for his trail. He couldn't stop and he couldn't go
on.

He shoved the pistol back into its holster. Carbine and canteen
bouncing against his sides, he managed a look behind. Three—no,
five—riders were galloping up the trail, the nearest perhaps a hundred yards away. That would have to do.

As the pony raced toward a bend in the trail, Faver swung his
off leg over the straining back. In the moment when looming rocks
screened him from his pursuers, he flung himself clear of the
horse, diving to land as far as possible from the trail.

He hit hard and rolled, carbine cradled in his arms. The impact
drove the air from his lungs in an agonized burst, and knife-edged
rocks ripped at his skin, but in a moment he was out of sight

among the boulders. Dimly, he heard his pony crashing away and, seconds later, the Apaches thundering past in pursuit. Then he was alone.

There hadn't been time to be afraid, and Faver didn't take time now. He wouldn't be alone for long. His trick wouldn't have fooled Nantahe or Chicuelo at all, and it wouldn't gain much time with this bunch. Faver rolled to his feet and ran downstream.

Just above the bend where he's first seen the two Apaches, he halted behind a screen of brush. There had been a lot of horses with the band, judging by the noise they'd made. They must still be there, guarded by a warrior or two. Faver reloaded his pistol. Maybe he wouldn't have to walk out, after all.

The canyon narrowed below the bend, trail and stream squeezed into a narrow slot at the far side. Two huge boulders, fallen long ago from the rim, blocked most of the opening. Loose earth and rocks had slid down over them, and past floods had piled logs and brush high on their sides. From the canyon beyond them, Faver heard the sounds of milling horses.

Moving swiftly, he clambered up the slide and snatched a look over the top. The boulders made a natural pocket on the downstream side, and a dozen skittish horses had been herded into it. A lone Apache sat his horse at the mouth of the depression. He had reined as near the sheer wall as possible, and the barrel of his rifle was steady on the bend in the trail.

Faver gauged his moment, scrambling across the top of the slide and out of sight while the guard's attention was on the herd. One short dash across the slide face would bring him to a clump of brush above the Indian. From there, a leap, a slash with his knife, and he could be on his way. It would hurt this band's pride to have their horses run off twice in one day.

The guard tucked the stock of his rifle under one arm, began to roll a cigarette. Too easy. Faver took the ten yards across the open in one smooth motion, went silently into the brush. He twisted to bring the carbine to bear, wondering if he could risk a shot.

Before he could move again, there was a shifting in the rocks above and behind him. He started to turn, but froze at the ratcheting click of a Springfield's hammer coming back to full cock. Then he knew.

"Hello, Nantahe," he said.

Knowing it was too late, he rolled to clear the carbine and tried to get off one shot. He'd barely started to move when something smashed into the side of his head, slamming him down into darkness.

CHAPTER 10

Faver woke first to the ache in his head, then to a racking pain between his shoulders. He opened his eyes and tried to sit up, but managed only to roll onto his side. His legs were free, but his arms had been yanked brutally behind him and bound at the elbows.

"Don't hurt yourself, white-eye. Lie still."

He had heard the mocking voice before, and the memory brought with it a cold dread. By hitching his body around, he brought the speaker into focus. It was an Apache, the same scarfaced warrior Faver had seen at the desert waterhole a few nights before. He sat cross-legged a couple of yards away, Faver's carbine across his lap. Behind him, Faver could see the scattered huts of the *ranchería*. No one else was in sight, but voices were speaking softly in Apache not far away.

"*Ai,* white-eye." Scar grinned at Faver, held up a small stick he'd been whittling on. "This is for you. You know?"

The peg was perhaps three inches long, sharpened to a needle point on either end. Faver closed his eyes, hoping the sudden spasm of nausea that gripped him would be put down to the blow on his head. He knew, all right. He'd seen such a peg before, had seen it used. The first time was when he was still young in the scouts, still learning.

The miners had made their camp near water, and the water had brought Nana's Apaches. Four whites died in the first rush, perhaps two days before Faver and Nantahe led the cavalry patrol in. Nantahe found the fifth, staked face-down on an anthill a half-mile from the camp. He knelt to examine the body, then straightened and stood looking down at it.

"What's wrong?" Faver asked.

Nantahe pointed. The miner's naked body was streaked with blood, but not enough to account for the crusted puddle by his head. Leaning closer, Faver saw the tensed, rigid jaw muscles and, finally, the sharpened stick, driven through the tongue and deep into the palate by the miner's convulsive efforts to close his mouth.

"God Almighty," Faver whispered. He drew back, the taste of sickness sharp in his throat. "No wonder they hate Apaches."

The skin of Nantahe's face was drawn tight, his cheekbones seeming to stand out more than usual. When he spoke, though, there was no expression in his voice or his eyes.

"I was thirteen by your count when the mob from Tucson hit Camp Grant. The People were camped there under the Army's protection. The men were away, hunting. I was with them."

Nantahe closed his eyes for a moment. "My sister was a year older. She was raped. Then her head was smashed with a rock. We found her, and about a hundred others, when we came home."

"But—" Faver shook his head, gestured helplessly at the thing on the ground. "Does it make this right? I don't understand."

"There's hate on both sides, and bad men. That's what we're fighting, Apache or white. That's what we have to stop." His teeth showed in a snarl. "And we'll stop this bunch, if they don't get us first."

Faver looked at the dead miner and shivered. "They'll never get me. Not like that."

The memory brought a surge of sweat-prickling fear to Faver, fear and something else. For all his big talk, they had him now. The cut-offs, the bad ones, had him, and Nantahe was one of them.

Faver felt a hot rush of shame and anger—shame at the weakness that made him afraid, anger at his own stupidity in underestimating an enemy who'd been a friend. And anger, too, at Nantahe, who had spoken his own big words, then ended by joining the murderers he claimed to despise.

In some cold corner of his mind, Faver realized that his anger was his only chance—slim enough, but all he had. He lashed it into a bitter rage, fed by the scarfaced Apache's mocking laughter. Then he heaved himself to a sitting position and looked at Scar.

The renegade was waiting, the wooden skewer still held between finger and thumb. He grinned again.

"You know, eh? What you think you'll do about that?"

"I'll send an owl to ride your chest in the night, fish-eater."

Most people would have seen no change in the renegade's face. Faver saw a parade of emotions—surprise at a captive who spoke fluent Apache, superstitious fear at the threat, rage at the insult. The Apache jumped to his feet, the carbine clattering unnoticed to the ground. He drew his knife and took a slow step toward Faver.

Ignoring the pain in his arms, Faver threw himself onto his back. He drew up his knees, ready to lash out with his heels. The warrior hesitated, then took another step.

"Don't do it, Scar. He'll kick your head in."

The guard whirled. So intent had he been on Faver that he hadn't noticed the sudden silence of the others, hadn't heard their approach from a nearby wickiup. Nantahe was in the lead. He was dressed in a checked shirt and ragged jeans, and his hair hung unbound to his shoulders. He carried a rifle negligently in the crook of his arm. Chicuelo came up on his right, looking at Faver with narrowed eyes, and five or six more warriors trailed along behind.

Scar sheathed his knife. "I want him," he said.

Nantahe didn't answer. He stepped closer to Faver, and now Faver could see the change in his face. He looked older. There were lines of strain around his mouth, a lurking something that was almost fear behind his eyes. It was a look Faver had seen before, on the faces of the renegades that he and Nantahe had hunted together.

"I knew you'd come," Nantahe said. "You couldn't stay north of the river and make it easy. I knew you'd follow."

Faver laughed. It didn't sound like much, coming from flat on his back, but he tried. "You always knew me better than I knew you, brother. I didn't think you'd take up with the kind of scum we used to pry from under rocks."

The other Apaches looked at Nantahe. "I want him." Scar said again.

Nantahe turned abruptly. "He's mine. I caught him, while you were chasing his horse." He shifted his hands slightly, and the rifle was pointing at Scar's chest. "Take him, if you think you can."

"Watch out, Nantahe." Chicuelo straightened, frowning. "Don't

90   RIDE DOWN THE WIND

do something stupid. You don't want to kill him slow, we'll kill him fast. But we better kill him."

Nantahe started to answer, but Faver cut in. Still speaking Apache, he aimed his words straight at Nantahe.

"He's right, brother." He kept his voice soft and controlled, as an Apache would, but he put a vicious emphasis on the last word. "You'd better kill me. Then you can pretend your word is still good, brother."

Nantahe came over to him, moving so that he didn't quite have to turn his back on Scar. Slowly, he shook his head.

"I'm not your brother. Not now. Your brother died when they chained him, when they stole his honor."

"Nobody stole your honor." It was easier for Faver to laugh this time, and the scorn in his voice was real. "You threw it away, along with your promise at the train. If there was any left, it stayed at a *rancho* north of here."

Nantahe's face went pale, and his hands tightened on the rifle. "Maybe I will kill you," he grated.

For a moment, Faver thought he'd gone too far. He felt an instant of bitter regret, but regret was a white man's emotion. He fought it down and waited, his face calm, his eyes steady on Nantahe.

Nantahe saw the change and understood it. He lowered the rifle.

"You learned," he said. "You learned a lot." He turned abruptly to the others. "That's all. We'll take him down to the road tonight and turn him loose."

"That's crazy," Chicuelo protested. "Why you want that kind of trouble? Kill him, now."

Nantahe didn't bother to answer. The older scout flushed angrily.

"Then I will!"

"No, you'll do what I say. He's mine. I owe him a life. If you want him, you'll have to fight me."

Chicuelo hesitated. The other Apaches exchanged glances, then backed away as if by common consent.

"You might kill me," Nantahe said very softly. "But who would watch your back, then? Scar?"

"Maybe." Chicuelo's voice was suddenly cautious, though. Nantahe pressed his advantage.

"Come on, *hombre*. We better talk about it. Nobody can start down that canyon before dark. We'll talk."

He walked back toward the hut he'd come from. One by one, the others followed, Scar stooping to pick up the Springfield. Chicuelo was last. He looked long and thoughtfully at Faver before turning away. Faver couldn't read the Apache's expression, but he doubted it meant anything good.

At first, he tried to hear what Nantahe and the others were saying, but their voices were only a murmur. They might have been arguing Nantahe's decision, or merely passing time. Either way, they spoke in the usual Apache fashion, quietly, one at a time, never interrupting.

He gave up after a time, rolled to a position that eased his arms a little, and tried to think. From what Nantahe had said, it seemed the scouts were clinging precariously to the leadership of the band. That made sense. Their training and experience would make them natural leaders here, but there would be some who were jealous, or angry at being displaced—and there would be a few like Scar, clinging like coyotes to the edge of any struggle, ready to pull down the weakest.

Without Nantahe and Chicuelo, the renegades could be beaten. One swift blow by Ordoñez and his troops would make them a rabble again, but the captain would have to be quick. Well, that was his problem. Faver's problem, at the moment, looked a little more serious.

He must have slept or fallen unconscious, because the next thing he knew, it was late afternoon and the valley floor was deep in shadow. He heard approaching footsteps and shook his head, trying to push back the throbbing pain.

"Get him up."

Faver caught his breath as rough hands hauled him upright. He tried to pull free, but Scar and another Apache held him in an unshakable grip. Nantahe and Chicuelo stood looking at him.

"You hear me?" Nantahe asked.

"I hear you."

"We owe you, Chicuelo and me," Nantahe said. Judging from Chicuelo's set face, Faver doubted that the older scout felt any great debt, but Nantahe was still speaking. "We owe you, and now we'll pay you. You gave us our lives at the train. We give back yours here."

He paused, waited a moment. Faver said nothing.

"Don't come back, Jess Faver," Nantahe said. "I'm just another Apache now, and you're just another white-eye. If I see you again, I'll kill you."

He looked at Faver a moment longer, then turned away.

"Chicuelo, see he gets to the road."

He walked away toward the wickiups. Chicuelo followed, then returned leading two horses. He murmured something to Scar, who mounted and sat waiting.

"Chicuelo." Nantahe had come back a few steps. "See he gets there alive, *compadre*. I don't want to kill you."

Chicuelo laughed sharply. He took down a lariat from one of the saddles and uncoiled it. "Alive," he agreed. "Just like we said. I don't want to kill you, either."

The rawhide lasso bit into the muscles of Faver's back and constricted his straining lungs until he gasped for air. Chicuelo had freed his arms and lashed his wrists together in front of him before they started, not out of mercy but because of Nantahe's warning. Faver grasped the rope with numbed hands, trying to take part of the strain on his arms as he stumbled down the trail.

The horses kept up a steady walk, moving at a pace just faster than a man—even a man not battered and exhausted as Faver was —could easily maintain. He was forced into a shambling half-trot, and more than once he fell on the rocky trail, tearing flesh and clothing and causing the rope to bite even deeper.

A wind had sprung up after sunset, lashing the tops of the creosote bushes, driving ahead of it gritty sand that lanced into Faver's unprotected arms and face. The journey seemed endless, but at last he felt the easing in his thighs and calves as the land leveled out. The mountains dropped away on either side, and the trail widened into a creek bed deep with sand. He knew the road couldn't be far ahead.

All at once, the pressure on his chest eased. He stumbled forward a few steps before he realized that the rope had gone slack. He stopped and raised his head.

Chicuelo and Scar had reined in their horses and were gazing down at him in the starlight. Unconsciously, Faver came erect, pulled his back straight and lifted his chin. Relief flooded through his muscles, and he drew new strength from it, until he stared back at the two Apaches with an arrogance that matched their own.

Chicuelo watched the transformation narrowly. After a moment, he smiled, a twist of his razor's-edge mouth that showed no hint of humor.

"We should have killed you," he said. "Nantahe is a fool."

Faver started to answer, but simple caution held him back. A wrong word now might still convince the scout to kill him, in spite of Nantahe's warning. He stood silently, flexing his bound arms in an effort to bring feeling back to his hands. His head still hurt, and Chicuelo's voice seemed to be coming from somewhere far away.

"Listen good, white-eye." The Apache urged his pony closer, looming over Faver. "Go back across the Río Bravo. Leave us alone." He pointed. "Go. The road is there."

Faver turned automatically to follow the gesture, his blurred senses registering no warning until it was too late, until Chicuelo hunched in the saddle and drove his heels into the pony's sides. The noose snapped tight across Faver's chest as the animal plunged forward. For an instant, he tried to brace against the strain, hands clutching vainly for the rope. Then he was snatched from his feet and hurled up a rocky, cactus-studded slope.

At first, he tumbled wildly, all control and sense of direction lost. The branches of a creosote bush lashed across his face and the warm taste of his blood sickened him. His hands found the rope, gripped it. With waning consciousness, he rolled to take the worst of the beating on his left side, protecting spine and belly and head.

Something stabbed at his groin. He jerked a leg up in blind reflex, and another something—a spur of rock, maybe—sliced through his jeans and deep into the muscle of his thigh. He dimly felt the pain of the wound, and the lesser pain as his teeth gashed his lower lip to hold in a scream.

It was too much, he knew, too much—he couldn't take it, and Chicuelo would have a hell of a lot of explaining to do when Nantahe found out.

Then there was a crushing blow on the left side of his head. The desert night exploded into a myriad of lights, and something in his left shoulder no longer supported him, and his fingers were slipping from the rope as he himself slipped down toward agony and silence and death. With the last strength that he had, Faver willed his fingers to stay clenched for one more second, one more instant, one more heartbeat, one more—

The mad wheeling of the stars stopped. Faver didn't realize what it meant, at first, didn't realize that rocks and branches no longer tore at him. Then he heard the soft crunch of moccasins on rocky ground. Rough hands grabbed his wrists, sending a fresh jolt through his injured shoulder. There was a quick yank, the sawing of a knife on rawhide cords, and his hands were free. Fingers groped along his back, and the bite of the noose went away.

"Well?" It was Chicuelo's voice. "Is he alive?"

The fingers grasped a handful of Faver's hair, pulled his head back. Through the mask of blood that gummed his eyelids, he looked up at Scar's wolfish grin.

"He's alive. You can tell Nantahe you did just like he said."

With complete determination, as if it were the most important thing in the world, Faver brought up his right hand, closed his fingers on Scar's wrist. The Apache looked down in surprise. Faver tried to speak, but gave it up. He had to say it all with his eyes, and with the animal snarl that twisted his bleeding mouth.

I'll see you again, he thought, straining to make the cut-off understand. You. I'll see you again. And I'll know you when I do.

Scar stared at him, then recovered. He twisted free and slammed Faver's face down into the dirt.

"Just like Nantahe said," he repeated with a harsh chuckle. He turned to mount his horse. "It's not our fault if the white-eye doesn't stay alive."

Faver never knew how long he lay there, hearing the hoofbeats fading until there was only the keening wind and the rasp of blown sand that flayed his raw skin. He lay on a gentle slope, his head slightly downhill, his face resting in the loose gravel of the hillside.

Chicuelo, motioning toward the road, had pointed downhill. Faver didn't know how far he'd been dragged, but he knew he would die if he stayed where he was, would die when the morning sun brought in a blistering, waterless day. Grimly, he clenched his fingers in the flinty soil and inched his body around. Sobbing aloud, his injured arm trailing beside him, Faver began to crawl.

The night resolved itself into an endless nightmare of tangled brush and tortured muscles, of agonized effort, of bleak periods of rest that only delayed the hopeless task of dragging his body downhill. With every fraction of excess strength, Faver concentrated, blocking out pain and fatigue by holding to a mounting hatred of Scar and Chicuelo, who had left him to die, and of Nantahe, who had sent them to do it. Through the long night, he clung to that hatred, until the hatred and the pain were the only things in the world for him.

Once, his outstretched hand touched only empty space and he tumbled headlong down a steep cutbank, hardly realizing that he had regained the creek bed and the trail. Another time, he was awakened from a fitful sleep by a snuffling and the thrust of a cold, wet muzzle against his cheek—or maybe that was a dream.

Finally, when the stars were pale and the sky gray with coming dawn, his hand found the deep, iron-hard wagon ruts of the road to La Morita. Some whisper of understanding penetrated the mists in his mind, and he relaxed the grip he'd held over himself for so long. A wave of weakness hit him, carried him into a dark place free from pain and the urgent need to crawl.

He didn't know when the wind died in predawn stillness. He didn't feel the warmth of the early sunrise, or hear the approaching riders, but even in his unconsciousness, even as gentle hands lifted him and bore him away, he clung to his hatred—the bleak, cold, murderous hatred of Nantahe and Chicuelo and Scar.

CHAPTER 11

He was inside a place that smelled of woodsmoke and people. The light was dim on his closed eyelids. His left hand and arm had no feeling, which worried him a little, but his right hand was free to move. His cautiously questing fingers touched the rough weave of a blanket on which he was lying.

Then, suddenly, they touched something else—the warmth and smoothness of flesh. Faver moved his arm ever so slightly, felt the shape of another body near him. He was not alone on the pallet.

In that moment, he remembered everything: the Apaches, the torture, his grim resolve to take vengeance. And Nantahe. Faver's jaw tightened, and his good hand clenched as though closing on a weapon. The slight movement sent pain flooding through his body, but he hardly noticed. If he was back in Nantahe's hands—

Then his control returned, gripping him in steel fingers. He couldn't be back among the Apaches. They were through with him, or thought they were.

The other person hadn't stirred at his touch, and Faver heard the sound of soft and regular breathing. Slowly, each movement adding a new increment of pain, he rolled to his right. For a moment, his vision was blurred. Then his sight cleared, and he looked into the sleeping face of Estella Alvarado.

She lay on top of the blankets, her black hair tousled, her face childish in sleep. Her left arm was stretched out toward Faver. The stays of her white blouse had come undone, and the softness of one brown breast pressed against the blanket.

Faver stared at her in uncomprehending wonder. He must have made some sound, for her lashes fluttered and she moaned softly in her sleep. Her eyes opened and she looked into his. She smiled sleepily. Then she was suddenly wide awake, her mouth open in astonishment. She flushed crimson and sprang to her feet, her hand darting to the throat of her blouse.

"You—you're awake," she whispered.

Faver tried to grin, gasped at the jolt of agony the motion sent through the side of his face. He automatically raised his hand, but Estella knelt and caught him by the wrist.

"No, wait," she said. "You have been hurt. Let me—let me call —Fernando, come quickly!"

The door of the little room crashed open and a man came through, filling the low doorway. He wore the white trousers and smock of a peasant, but a heavy gunbelt circled his waist and he held a pistol in one huge hand. He looked uncertainly at Faver and the girl, then holstered the weapon with a sheepish smile.

"I thought there was trouble, *señorita*. You should not scream. So, he's awake at last."

"At last?" Faver spoke in a normal tone, and instantly regretted it. He tried again, keeping his voice down and trying not to move his lips. "At last? How long has it been? And how did I get here?"

And where was here, anyway, he added to himself. He realized he had a lot of questions. He'd been unconscious, but there were snatches, like a dream, where he was hunting Nantahe, where they were fighting, sometimes with knives. But in his dream, someone had held him back.

He looked up at Estella again. She dropped her eyes, the color burning on her cheeks.

"It has been four days since we found you on the road," Fernando said. "Paco came to us for help, as the friends of his father, and by good luck and the Virgin, we found you alive."

"Four days," Faver murmured.

"You were out of your head, with fever and—" The big man hesitated, glanced at Estella. "—and something worse, perhaps. We sent for the *señorita,* and for a *curandero* to help you." He grinned. "But I think maybe the *señorita* was the best medicine."

"Fernando, pig!" Estella advanced on him. "Get out, oaf! Find Tío Jorge and send him in, if you can say nothing sensible. Go!"

Fernando retreated to the door, laughing. "Watch her, *gringo,*" he advised Faver. "Now that you're awake, you'll find she has a temper."

He ducked as Estella grabbed for something to throw. Still laughing, he pulled the door closed and went away.

"Pig," Estella repeated.

She stared at the closed door for a moment, then turned. Faver was watching her.

"He is a joker, a clown," she said defensively. "You must not listen to him."

Faver shook his head. He was careful not to smile. "No. I remember, now. Some of it, anyway. Thank you."

"It was nothing. And you had saved Paco." She came suddenly and sat beside him, looking into his eyes. "But you said such—such terrible things. You talked of killing and killing, and in such ways—" She shuddered and bowed her head. "I don't like to think of it."

Faver reached out to take her hand. Every movement still cost him pain, but the weakness that had worried him at first seemed to be passing.

"I was out of my head," he said, intensely conscious of the girl's nearness. Unbidden, the picture of her sleeping came back to him. "*Loco*. I didn't mean whatever I said."

She shook her head, drew back from him a little. "No, it wasn't just the fever." She hesitated, then said, "It was as though you were—another person. Someone like—"

Like an Apache, Faver finished silently. Estella broke off, jumping to her feet as the door opened again. An old man in peasant's clothing came in, carrying a basket. Fernando started to follow, then glanced at Estella and stopped in the open doorway. The old man came to Faver's pallet in a brisk hobble, smiled down at him.

"Ah, *bueno*. Fernando said you were awake. Now you will live."

Faver swallowed. "That's good," he said.

"This is Tío Jorge," the girl explained. "He is our *curandero*. There is no doctor in—here."

"I know something of herbs. And other things," Tío Jorge said modestly. "Now the *señorita* must leave, and I will dress your hurts."

Fernando chuckled. "There is little she could see that would surprise her," he said.

He ducked backward, but the expected explosion didn't come. Estella shot him a disdainful look, then marched from the room. The color was back in her cheeks, but she kept her chin high and her eyes steady. Faver thought she was beautiful in that moment, proud and straight as an Apache girl, but with a softness the Apaches lost very young.

"Now, you will see." Tío Jorge put out a calloused hand and drew back the blanket. "For a time, you were *muy malo*, very bad. Now it is better."

It was bad, but not as bad as Faver had feared. As the bandages came off, he saw that they covered cuts and abrasions and the purplish-green swellings of old bruises. There was a bone-deep gash in his right thigh, clean and already closing with spongy scar tissue, and the scars of many lesser wounds on his back and legs.

Tío Jorge inspected the damage cheerfully, with many clucking sounds of satisfaction. At last, he began replacing the bandages, first smearing them with a foul-smelling mixture of herbs and grease.

"It all goes well," he said. "You have great strength. Only this is still a problem."

His square hands touched Faver's left shoulder gently. The arm and shoulder were heavily plastered with poultices made from some leaf Faver didn't recognize, and a splint immobilized the joints.

"I have some small skill with broken bones. You will, I think, get back its use, but not for many days. But it should not hurt you greatly while the poultice is there."

"I—" Faver began, then stopped. He raised a hand to the side of his face. "What about this?"

The old man went to a table on the far side of the room, returned with a cloudy hand mirror. Wordlessly, he held it out. Faver turned it, squinting, until he could see his face more or less clearly.

Above a scraggly beard, his eyes stared back from deep hollows. There was an egg-shaped swelling over his left cheekbone, with some puffiness and discoloration remaining from what must have been a beautiful black eye. A raw scab ran from the corner of his mouth back to someplace below his ear. He remembered the slash across his face and the taste of blood, and knew he'd carry that scar to his grave.

"You're still weak." Tío Jorge took a battered tin cup from the table and poured something into it from a bottle. "Can you drink?"

Faver accepted the cup almost without thinking and took a long swallow. He got half of it down, then choked, coming half-erect in the bed. Fernando hurried across to help him.

"Good night!" Faver glared at the murky contents of the cup. "What is that stuff?"

"A tea made from popotillo leaves and a little goat blood. It will build your strength. Drink it."

Faver shuddered, but raised the cup again and drained it. "Anything that tastes like that is bound to give you strength." He handed the cup back to Tío Jorge. "Now, I'd like to talk to Captain Ordoñez. Can you ask him to come here?"

Tío Jorge and Fernando exchanged glances, and Fernando smiled.

"Not today, *hombre*. You get some rest first. Then you can see the *jefe,* and maybe the *señorita* again."

Tío Jorge rearranged the blankets and left, promising to come again the next day. Faver tried to question Fernando, but he was getting drowsy, and the big man wasn't inclined to talk. He went out, finally, leaving Faver puzzled.

Something was being hidden from him, something they didn't want him to know or hadn't decided how to handle. He had no idea what it could be, and after a few moments he decided he didn't care. He needed to rest and regain his strength. Then, in time, he had to go after Nantahe.

Nantahe. Chicuelo. Scar. They mattered. Beyond that, nothing could be too important.

Three days passed before Estella Alvarado came again. She entered the little room not long after Tío Jorge had finished his daily call. Seeing Faver sitting up on the cot, she smiled.

"You're better. We were so worried for those first days."

He looked ruefully at the leaves that still plastered his left shoulder. Most of the other bandages were gone. The bruises were fading and the cuts healing, leaving his back and chest ridged with scars like the marks of a whip.

"I'm fine," he said. "Tío Jorge says I can get up in a couple more days, but I think I could make it sooner." He grinned, watching her. "Then you'll have to tell me where I am."

The girl caught her breath. She started to protest, but Faver had seen enough in her face to tell him he was right. He cut in firmly.

"No, I figured it out the other day. Everybody was just a little too careful about what they said. This isn't La Morita."

Estella hesitated, then shook her head. "No. It is another village, south of La Morita and higher in the mountains."

There was a window, glassless and heavily shuttered, in one wall of the shack. She crossed to it, fumbled with the wooden fasteners for a moment, then pushed back the shutters. Faver blinked in the unexpected rush of light. Outside, he could see a cluster of adobe *jacales,* with the ruined tower of a mission church rising in the background. The high wall of a cliff rose behind the buildings to block out the sky.

"When Paco rode for help that night, he came to the closest place where he knew he could find friends. He—" Again the hesitation. "We have relatives here."

"And how about Captain Ordoñez? Does he have relatives here? Does he know I'm alive?"

Estella looked at the floor. "No," she whispered. "No one knows in La Morita, except for Paco and me."

Faver grinned. "I'll bet your boss, Señor Braswell, knows," he said. "Ordoñez told me you lived with your aunt and uncle in the village. Where do they think you are?"

She straightened abruptly, all confusion gone. "I go where I please," she snapped. Then she took a step toward him, holding out her hand in appeal. "If we had tried to take you to La Morita, you might have died. What could we do?"

"You did enough. More than I could have expected."

Almost without thinking, Faver reached to capture her extended hand. She came to him easily, her eyes wide with surprise—surprise at his action and, perhaps, at her own sudden lack of will. Then his good hand was at the back of her neck, her long hair trickling past his fingers. He drew her down until she knelt with one knee on the edge of the cot and her lips were soft on his.

For a moment, she leaned into him breathlessly and returned the kiss. Then her brown eyes opened suddenly and she pulled away.

"No, I—Luis would—I can't." She brushed aimlessly at the front of her skirt. "I think you are well. Maybe it's time for you to meet the *jefe*, the chief."

She almost ran from the room. Faver rubbed his chin absently, trying to be angry with himself. He knew he'd made a mistake. He had no right to get involved with this girl, nothing to offer her. There were things he had to do, and she could only be in the way.

"All right," he murmured finally. "Let's meet the *jefe*."

The *jefe* was a small man. His stooped shoulders seemed too frail to support the bandolier of ammunition that hung across his chest, and his waist seemed too lean for the weight of the pistol in his belt. He had a receding chin and a fierce, bristling moustache that completely hid his mouth. There was nothing impressive about him, not even his muddy brown eyes. They studied Faver closely, but there was something curiously flat about them, as if a shutter behind the pupils kept anyone from looking too deep.

"Well, *gringo*," he greeted Faver, "Tío Jorge told me you were starting to ask questions. I should have come sooner."

"You found me? After the Apaches—left me?"

"*Sí*. I and a few of my boys."

"Yeah. Thanks."

The little man waved it away. "*De nada*. You have saved Paco, the child of Esteban Alvarado. We are in your debt." He paused thoughtfully. "But now there is a problem."

"I don't doubt it," Faver said. "You're Zamora?"

The bandit leader drew himself erect and his moustache twitched with a hidden smile.

"Ah, you know of me! Felix Zamora del Porrena, at your service."

"Jess Faver," Faver said dryly. He extended a hand, and Zamora shook it reluctantly.

"You understand my problem, *gringo*. There are few outsiders who know about this place, and fewer still who know of our—ah—connection with Señor Braswell. You're welcome here, as my guest. But some of my boys—I mean no offense, *hombre*—don't think you can be trusted."

Zamora didn't sound especially worried about what his men thought, but even a bandit chief, Faver reflected, had to keep his troops happy. He could understand Zamora's feelings well enough.

"Then I'm a prisoner here, not a guest."

Zamora chuckled, but there was no change in his flat brown eyes. He touched the bandage on Faver's shoulder.

"You won't be able to leave for a while. Stay as Zamora's guest. We'll have plenty of time to decide whether you're Zamora's prisoner."

If he was a prisoner, it was a comfortable and even enjoyable imprisonment. In a few days, he was on his feet, feeling wobbly as a new colt. He could feel his strength returning daily as his body healed, but there were other, deeper wounds that did not heal.

After a few curious glances, the bandits and their women accepted Faver as part of the landscape. He began to walk through the village and up the canyon beyond, a little farther each day. Except for the sling on his left arm, he felt almost as good as new by the time of the girl's next visit.

Faver had just left his quarters when the trader's wagon drove into the village, surrounded by an escort of mounted bandits. The driver reined in the team in the village square and Estella swung down from the wagon box. She started for his hut, then saw him standing outside. Smiling, she ran lightly to meet him.

"Should you be out here?" There was concern in her voice. "Perhaps you should be resting, or—" She saw him laughing at her and interrupted herself with a little shake of her head. "I'm sorry. I sound like a—like my Aunt Concepción."

"You don't look like her," Faver said. He pointed up the canyon. "I was going for a walk. Come with me."

In the shade of the high rock wall, there was a trickle of water that fed into the village cistern. Estella took Faver's arm quite naturally, and he led her along the grassy bank beside the stream until a turn hid the village. There she stopped and turned to face him expectantly.

The invitation was clear enough in her serious brown eyes, but this time he didn't take it. He'd hardly given her a conscious thought since he'd last seen her, but he realized now how much he'd come to depend on her visits. That was bad. He couldn't afford to depend on anyone here, least of all a pretty girl confusing gratitude with something stronger. It was time for him to back away.

"Being out on that wagon is dangerous, with the Apaches acting up," he said, a little more roughly than he'd intended. "I'm surprised the captain lets you do it."

She looked up at him, surprised. "I told you, I do as I wish."

"Ordoñez told me you were going to marry him."

"Oh." She dropped her hand from his arm and stepped back a little, but her eyes didn't leave his face. "Yes. Luis wants me to marry him, to go back to Ciudad Mexico with him when he is transferred."

"Yeah." Faver raised his eyebrows. "The captain—how much does he know about you and"—he waved his arm in a gesture that took in the canyon, the village, and all of Zamora's bunch—"and this?"

"He doesn't know. He would be very shocked, because he hates the bandits." Her eyes darkened. She hesitated, then said softly, "It isn't quite the way you think with me. Luis wishes to marry me. But no—no man from La Morita would think of me in that way."

Faver grinned. "That's hard to believe," he said.

"No." She almost smiled, but not quite. "I don't mean that. It is my parents, my mother." She paused again, went on quickly. "She was from the city, from Chihuahua. She was never happy here. When Papa died, she couldn't stay. There was a foreman at Don Gonzalo's ranch, and they—she—went away with him."

Tears gleamed in Estella's eyes, but she looked at him defiantly.

"She meant to send for Paco and me. I know she did."

"Nobody could blame you—" Faver began, but he realized how stupid it sounded. Certainly, people could blame her. It happened every day in the States; why should it be different here?

"When I was old enough, I took the job with Señor Braswell. I knew people would think I was"—she blushed—"well, his woman. But I didn't care. I couldn't stay with my aunts and hear them talk about my mother. Tía Concepción—she is the wife of the blacksmith in town—she does not judge so quickly. I live there now."

Faver nodded. The girl seemed very young and fragile, standing motionless in front of him, but he was beginning to believe she wasn't nearly as fragile as she looked.

"Is that how you got mixed up with Zamora?" he asked. "Through the job?"

"Oh, no. Señor Braswell gave me the job because of Fernando. He is a cousin, I think, to my father and his people. Tío Ramón, who was killed at the *rancho,* gave Fernando information sometimes, and hid him once when the *federales* were after him."

She laughed at Faver's surprised expression.

"They were family," she said, as if that explained it all, and perhaps it did. "But I think Zamora doesn't trust me quite so much, since Luis wants to marry me."

Faver hesitated, aware suddenly of the world around them, of the canyon and the soft splash of water and the glare of the sun.

"Is that what you want, too?" he asked.

She was silent for a moment. Then she raised her head and looked steadily into his face.

"It was," she said. When he didn't answer, she turned away, not quite quickly enough to hide the hurt in her eyes. "Come. We must go back."

This time, she walked ahead of him, her back proudly straight. Faver followed, not speaking until they came back to the village. She didn't understand what was in his mind, and he couldn't tell her.

His body might heal, but he still awoke in the night to the stabbing pain in his shoulder. He still dreamed of branches ripping at his flesh and the wheeling dance of the stars and the laughter of Chicuelo and Scar. Those memories were burned deep into him, deeper than any scars he bore. He knew they could only be wiped away with blood.

CHAPTER 12

Zamora's hut was a little larger than the others, but outwardly that was the only difference. Two hard-faced bandits lounged on a bench beside the doorway, staring coldly at Faver as he knocked on the door.

"*Sí*. Come."

Zamora was sitting at a field desk almost like the one in Ordoñez' office. He glanced up as Faver entered, then rolled the map he'd been studying and shoved it into one of the pigeonholes.

"*Bueno, gringo*. Thank you for coming."

"I didn't know I had a choice."

"You look better." Zamora waved him to a seat, then turned his head to call through an inside doorway. "Carmel! Carmelita, *guapa*, bring us a drink."

Faver sank into the surprisingly comfortable chair and leaned back, looking around the room. A dark-haired girl, pretty and much younger than Zamora, came from what Faver supposed was the kitchen, bringing a bottle and two glasses. She set them on the edge of the desk, then straightened and smiled boldly at Faver. Zamora chuckled.

"No, *chiquita*, this one isn't for you. Not yet, anyway. Leave us, now."

She pouted and went, closing the door. Zamora splashed whiskey into the glasses, drank his in a gulp.

"Your friends are causing us much trouble," he said. "They hit some of my boys last night."

"Apaches?" Faver was on his feet at once, his voice eager. "Where? How many?"

The bandit leader's moustache twitched with his hidden smile. "I don't know how many. The boys were down by the Chihuahua road, waiting for a gold shipment. The *cabróns* wounded two, and ran off their horses."

"It's getting so a man can't make an honest living," Faver murmured. He saw Zamora's suspicious glance and went on quickly. "Maybe I can do something about the Apaches. But I have to get out of here first."

Zamora leaned back, drumming his fingers on the desk top.

"Back to La Morita and *el capitán?* We have enough troubles, without the soldiers learning where you've been."

"I don't have to tell them," Faver said tightly. "In fact, I don't have to go back. Give me a horse and a gun, and I'll finish my business in the hills."

"Maybe. But maybe we're only out a horse and a gun. Guns are hard to come by, *gringo.*"

"I thought my credit was good."

Zamora shrugged. "You saved Paco. We saved you. Everything's even, no?"

Faver almost laughed. Nantahe had told him the same thing, there at the Apache camp, just before Scar and Chicuelo had gotten hold of him. The bandit leader might have something similar in mind, but he'd probably figure on making it permanent.

Caught by the memory, Faver almost missed Zamora's next words.

"It is a problem. Now, if you decided to join us—"

Zamora let his voice trail off thoughtfully, his flat brown eyes intent on Faver. Faver was surprised, but caution and long habit kept his face blank.

"Yeah? What if I did?"

"I could use a man like you, *gringo.* You know how to fight, and how to train others. And you know your way around north of the river, no?"

Faver nodded. The little bandit poured himself another drink, turned the glass in his hands.

"There's much gold to be made, *gringo.*" He chuckled and jerked his head toward the kitchen door. "Gold and other things, maybe better. We can help you get your revenge, it that's what you want, and maybe you can help us."

"I'll think about it," Faver said.

Zamora's eyes narrowed. "Your arm," he said abruptly. "It is all right, now?"

Faver loosened the sling a little, raised his left arm, grimacing with just a bit more pain than he actually felt.

"Tío Jorge says a few days, yet. It'll be strong soon."

"*Bueno*. You think on what I say, until the sling comes off. Then you can decide."

He nodded to show the audience was over, reached to take out the map again. Faver rose to leave, but the bandit's voice stopped him at the door.

"*Gringo?*" Zamora didn't raise his eyes from the map. "*Gringo,* don't think too long."

Outside, Faver stood for a moment. Tío Jorge had said the arm would be slow in mending, but he couldn't afford to wait. He'd have to do something, and soon.

"You, *hombre!*" One of Zamora's guards advanced, scowling. "The boss is through with you. Move on—*¿Cómo?*"

Faver grinned at him, commented on his ancestry in Apache, and walked away. Almost without thinking, he turned his steps toward Fernando's hut. Estella had chosen not to go back to La Morita after their meeting in the canyon. Instead, she was staying with Fernando's woman and children.

"What will—your aunt think, when you don't come back?" Faver had asked.

"My Aunt Rosa lives on a farm near here. I sent word by the wagon driver that I was staying a few days with her." She lowered her long lashes. "To think things over."

"It must be handy to have that many aunts."

He'd left it at that. He wasn't sure what her motive was, but it had been her choice, and he was glad to have someone around he could trust.

Estella was standing with her back to the open door. She had hung a dress on the front of a big wooden cabinet in one corner of the room, and she was brushing at it with a damp cloth. She looked around as his shadow fell across the doorway.

"Oh! I didn't want you to see."

Teresa, Fernando's plump, bouncy wife, was rolling out tortillas on a table beside the room's big fireplace. She laughed and waved Faver inside.

"I'm glad you're here, *gringo*. This one has been worrying about her dress all day." She winked slyly at Faver. "Maybe now she'll think of something else."

Estella made a face at her. "It's just that I'm tired of looking like a field hand." She turned to Faver, excitement lighting up her face. "Teresa says the men will be back from the *río* soon—maybe today. Then there will be a *baile,* with food and dancing and many presents."

"From the *río?*" Faver knew that a dozen of the bandits had ridden out a few days before, driving a herd of cattle—stolen cattle, he supposed. "They went to trade, then?"

"Yes, and when they return, there'll be a party, so I was readying the dress. But now you've spoiled it."

"Maybe not," he said. He took her arm. "Let's walk up the canyon. I want to show you something."

Teresa giggled. When Faver looked her way, she turned her back and bent busily to her work. Estella started to say something, but he stopped her with a quick shake of his head. Half angrily, she pulled a shawl around her shoulders and marched ahead of him out the door.

Neither spoke until they reached the edge of the village. Then Estella stopped abruptly.

"Now, what is this great thing you want to show me? And if you're so concerned about my marriage, why did you leave Teresa thinking—"

"Never mind Teresa," he interrupted firmly. "Look. Back by that last *jacal*. That hard case rolling a cigarette."

"So? What about him?"

Faver led her on up the canyon. "He was one of the guards outside Zamora's place. He's following me." He kept a tight grip on her arm as she started to turn. "No, don't look back. We can talk by the stream."

"But why should anyone follow you? You're a guest here."

"Your friend Zamora is having second thoughts about me. If I'd join his bunch, or go back north for good, it might be all right. But he's afraid to turn me loose, knowing as much as I do."

The girl lowered her eyes. "And you don't wish to leave here—for good?"

"I have something to finish." Then, seeing the hurt in her face, "Estella, after that—" He hesitated, shrugged. "¿Quién sabe? But Zamora has to do something. If I wait long enough, he'll have me killed."

"Killed?" Estella's voice rose with shock. She glanced nervously behind them, then went on more softly. "But he wouldn't! Fernando loves Paco like his own, and there are others, relatives of Tío Ramón, who are grateful to you. They wouldn't allow it."

They had reached an open stretch of canyon, where neither rocks nor brush provided enough cover to hide a man within forty or fifty yards. Faver stopped and put his back against the cool rock wall. It seemed natural for him to take Estella's hand—the bandit following him would expect him to do something, at least—so he did.

"I don't mean he'd 'dobe wall me, Estella. He's too smart an old fox for that. But if I got knifed during a card game, or killed in a fight over what somebody said about you"—he grinned at her, and she blushed—"nobody could blame Zamora."

"Oh." She was silent for a moment. "What can we do?"

"We need to talk." He had his shadow spotted, behind a spur of rock maybe forty yards away. It should be far enough, but he had cause to know how sound could carry between these rock walls. "If we can find a place where we're sure nobody can hear us—"

The girl laughed softly. She stepped into him, pulling his good arm around her shoulders, her eyes sparkling with mischief.

"Now he can't hear us," she whispered, lips close against his neck. "This is what he's been waiting to see, anyway."

"But—" Faver started to protest, then changed his mind. "The bandits coming back from selling the cattle." He had a little trouble keeping his attention on what he wanted to say. "They'll have money. Will Braswell's wagon be coming in to trade?"

"Yes, they'll come. Señor Braswell always sends them, whenever—"

"Whenever there's a nickel to be made. Hey, look out. That's—"

Estella laughed again, a little breathlessly. "Don't squirm. You're supposed to be enjoying this. Just tell me what we're going to do."

The bandits who had taken the herd north returned early the next day, whooping and firing their guns into the air. Their leader waved a canvas bag over his head.

"Gold, *jefe!* The *Tejanos* paid in gold!"

The sentries had seen them coming long before, and preparations for the *baile* had already begun. Goats and a steer were slaughtered and spitted to cook over open beds of coals. Half a dozen men hauled up a cart loaded with water jars to sprinkle the dust of the plaza. Women kneaded flat loaves of bread, or unearthed hoarded sugar to make *dulces*. And men and women alike brought out their best clothing for the party.

Braswell's wagon creaked into the village that afternoon. The driver and guards unharnessed the horses and made camp a short distance below the village, sending for Estella to keep the books for the trading. They unloaded high-piled bales of drying candelilla, uncovering the goods hidden beneath: sugar, salt and flour, bolts of cloth, cases of whiskey and wine, dozens of other items. There were no guns, Faver noted, and very little ammunition.

"A new rifle will bring its weight in silver," Estella told him. "The soldiers on both sides of the river watch closely for arms. Even Señor Braswell can't bring in many."

Toward sundown, fires were built in the plaza. A band gathered at one side—guitars and fiddles, and one skinny old man with a trumpet. The women served food, and a great deal of the whiskey brought by the wagon was drunk. Zamora, wearing a tall black sombrero piped with silver, held court in front of his quarters, while his whole gang seemed to be crowded into the plaza.

A procession of bandits came one after the other, respectfully asking Estella to dance. Faver danced with half a dozen of the women, from Fernando's laughing Teresa to the brazen, dark-eyed girl he'd seen in Zamora's hut.

"I'll make a dress of this," she'd said, pulling a length of green-and-gold cloth from one of the bolts bought that day. "Do you like it? I'll wear it for you."

To anyone watching, it would have seemed that Faver drank quite a lot. When he finally reclaimed Estella, they quarreled in low tones, then made up. He leaned close and whispered to her. She shook her head, pushing him away, but gradually she weakened. It was nearly midnight when he staggered to his feet, cradling a bottle in the crook of his injured arm, and drew her off into the darkness. One or two of the outlaws called drunken advice or encouragement after them, but the others seemed too busy to notice.

As soon as he and Estella were outside the glow of the fires, Faver yanked the sling free and threw it away. He flexed his left arm and swore.

"How about our friend? I didn't see him when we left."

The girl tossed her head. "He was talking to that Carmelita cat earlier. They were dancing."

"I hope she took him someplace quiet," Faver muttered. "The wagon's this way. Come on."

Arms about each other's waists, they moved down the rutted path. They stopped frequently, and once Faver drew her aside into the shadow of a *jacal*. She cuddled against him, giggling, while he searched the darkness behind them. There were other couples nearby, talking, laughing, or pressing together in urgent silence.

"Well?" Estella whispered finally. "Have you forgotten why we came?"

"Not quite. I guess we've lost him. How about Braswell's men?"

"There should be one guard, unless he's given up and joined the *baile* by now."

When they came within sight of the wagon, the guard was still there, squatting in the light of a small fire. He glanced wistfully toward the sound of the guitars, and Faver ducked back behind the corner of a building.

"Wide awake, and he's got a rifle. Looks like he's been drinking, but not enough to help."

Estella wrinkled her nose at him. "Do we give up, then? Carmelita might save you another dance."

"No, thanks." He took another quick look. "I'll work around the wagon, come up behind him. Do you think you can make him look the other way for a minute?"

She laughed, loudly and clearly. Before Faver realized what she was doing, she plucked the bottle from his hand and rounded the corner into the firelight.

The guard jumped to his feet, rifle ready. When he saw Estella, he hesitated, then laid the gun aside with a sheepish smile. She laughed again and moved toward him.

"*Ai, hombre.*" Her voice was low and husky. "So brave, to stand guard while the others play. Perhaps you're lonely here, yes?"

Faver shook himself, then circled quickly behind the building to come up on the far side of the wagon. He had no reason to be surprised, he reminded himself. There was clearly a lot he still didn't know about Estella Alvarado.

He wasn't sure which way the guard would be facing, so he took the shortest route, scrambling under the high bed of the wagon to materialize almost at the man's elbow. The guard broke off a passionate kiss with Estella, struggled an instant against her pinioning arms, then tore free. His hand dived for the knife at his belt.

Faver willed his left to swing hard and low, but the arm didn't quite get the message. He caught the man with a glancing blow in the ribs, then rocked him back against the wagon with a straight right to the face. It wasn't enough to jar loose the knife, but it threw the guard off balance. He swept the knife up in a round-house arc, but before it could connect, Faver's boot socketed into his groin with agonizing force.

The sentry doubled over, gasping. Faver sidestepped and clubbed his right forearm down across the back of his opponent's neck. The man went down, flat on his face in the dirt.

"You have killed him?"

Estella was back against the wagon. She had picked up the rifle. Faver glanced at her, then knelt and pressed his hand to the guard's back.

"He's all right. He'll be asleep for a while, though."

"Good." She scrubbed vigorously at her lips with the back of her hand. "The horses, now."

"Yes, ma'am," Faver muttered. Aloud and in Spanish, he said, "Give me the rifle. You might look for some food and blankets to take along."

She swung up onto the wagon box. Grinning wryly, Faver propped the unconscious guard against the rear wheel, then walked down to the picket line. At least he was learning a trade, he thought. If he ever got home, he could always become a horse thief.

An hour before sunup, Faver reined in the horses and dismounted. Estella was half asleep in her saddle, numb with exhaustion and shivering in the predawn cold. She hardly raised her head when he reached to help her down.

"There's a *jacal* and a barn," he whispered. "I think they're deserted. Wait here while I look. *¿Comprende?*"

She nodded, clutching automatically at the reins he thrust into her hands. Since taking the horses, they had ridden south to the road, then east toward La Morita, then south again along a barely visible trail leading into the hills. They'd put a lot of miles between themselves and the bandits, and it was doubtful that Zamora could track them if he tried.

Faver made a quick scout of the area and was back in minutes.

"Looks safe enough. We'll rest here." He unstrapped their gear from the saddles and gave the bundles to the girl. "Wait inside. I'll put the horses in the barn."

He expected to find her asleep when he came in from tending the animals, but she was slicing bread and dried meat by the light of a guttering candle. A fire glowed in the tiny corner fireplace, and he rubbed his hands in front of it.

"Just like home," he said, and Estella smiled.

Sitting on the floor, he examined his new rifle carefully. It was a lever-action Marlin, clean and well tended. It would have a better rate of fire than his lost Springfield, but less range and stopping power. He wondered if it was a good trade.

Estella held out a thick sandwich to him, and he laid the rifle aside. "Thanks." He bit into it hungrily, then looked up at her. She was awake now, plainly tired, but with a lot of reserves left.

"We must decide what to do," she said.

"Well, we can't go into La Morita together. What would Luis say?"

She didn't smile. "He thinks you're dead. Most of the people do." She knelt beside him, her face serious. "You will have to tell them something. The *bandidos*—even Zamora—are my people, my kin. You mustn't lead the soldiers to them."

Faver shook his head. "Don't worry. My quarrel isn't with

Zamora." Not yet, he added to himself. But no one, bandit or captain, had better get in his way when he went after Nantahe. "What about you?"

She shrugged. "Luis—everyone—thinks I'm visiting my Aunt Rosa. I'll stay with her for a day or two, then come back." She didn't meet his eyes. "If that is how you wish it," she added softly.

"That's good," Faver said. He stood up and stretched. "We'd better get some sleep. It's getting light outside."

He spread a blanket in one corner of the room and sat on it to pull off his boots. He leaned back against the wall, the rifle propped within easy reach. Estella blew out the candle and sat beside him, pulling her blanket over them both. After a moment, she leaned closer, resting her head against his chest.

"Jess?" she murmured sleepily. "The way I acted. I am not that way, not really. I'm sorry."

Faver put his arm around her shoulders, touched her hair. In spite of his resolutions, his body ached for her with a hunger that fought against his weariness.

His debt to Nantahe had started as a simple thing between the two of them. Then its consequences had spread, like ripples spreading when a stone was dropped into a pond. The ripples had touched Estella, and now she was a part of it all.

Those ripples were still spreading. They seemed likely to finish in fire and death, and Faver didn't mean to draw her deeper with him.

The girl stirred and whispered something in her sleep. Faver sat still, cradling her body against his chest, looking down into her face as the fire died in the little room and light grew in the sky outside.

CHAPTER 13

Faver rode into La Morita late in the afternoon. He'd seen Estella safely to her aunt's place in the hills, then turned back toward town. He wasn't looking forward to explaining his long absence to Ordoñez, but he would just have to live with that problem. Before he could start after Nantahe, he would need supplies and a secure base to work from. La Morita was his best bet.

The road was far more crowded than he'd seen it before. He passed wagons and high-wheeled *carretas,* peasants leading donkeys, whole families trooping on foot toward the village, hurrying as the sun sank lower. The narrow streets of the town itself were made even narrower by a tangle of tents and lean-to shelters, temporary quarters for people running scared. Faver had been out of touch with the outside world during his weeks in the bandit camp. Now he read all he needed to know of the Apache raids in the faces of the villagers as he passed.

The square was crowded. It was market day, and stalls had been set up in the open space before Braswell's store. Baskets of corn and squash and beans filled some of the booths, while others offered trussed and squawking chickens, woven blankets—more things than he could take in at a glance. Buyers and sellers haggled in the open. Children played around the fringes of the crowd, and old men gathered to watch and gossip on the porch of the store.

"*¡Madre de Dios!*" An old woman who fried and sold tortillas filled with beans was the first to notice Faver. She stood frozen, her wares forgotten. Her first shrill cry caused other heads to turn, and silence spread like a wave through the plaza. Women pulled shawls over their shoulders and crossed themselves, and the men moved together into little knots, eyeing him warily. The soldier on duty at the Guardia barracks took one startled look and bolted inside.

Faver didn't understand. He heard the sound of his horse's hooves as he reined him toward the barracks, heard the yelp of a stray dog loud in the tense quiet. The concentrated weight of a hundred pairs of eyes bore down on him. He dismounted in front of the captain's office and tied the horse. His hand touched the rifle in its scabbard, but he drew back. He couldn't tell if the crowd was hostile or not, but the gun wouldn't help much if it was.

A man detached himself from one of the nearest groups and came toward Faver. He was big and bearded, bearing a resemblance to Fernando, but with an even greater depth of chest and shoulder. He wore a grimy leather apron over his white peasant's garb.

"I—I am Valentín Guerrero," he said. His voice was deep and quiet, but it held a hint of uncertainty, almost of fear. "I am the uncle by marriage of the boy Paco."

Faver stepped out to meet him, saw him draw back involuntarily. This was Tía Concepción's husband; Estella had mentioned he was a blacksmith. But why was everyone staring as if—

Suddenly, Faver understood. He'd been away for almost two months, with only Paco and Estella knowing he was alive. As far as the townspeople were concerned, he'd died in the hills. No wonder his appearance was a surprise to them.

"I'm Jess Faver," he said quietly. Unsmiling, he extended his hand. "Pleased to meet you, *señor*."

Slowly, Guerrero put out a work-hardened hand. His fingers touched Faver's, clamped down. Then, without warning, Faver found himself caught up in a bone-crushing *abrazo* by the blacksmith's huge arms. In the same instant, the silence shattered into a babble of excited speech: "It's him. The *gringo*. Blessed saints, he's alive!" and, in lower tones, "His face! Look what they've done to him."

Finally releasing his grip, Guerrero stepped back. Faver was astonished to see that the big man was almost in tears.

"Estella always said you would be alive. She knew. We have kept your horse, and now you must—" He broke off suddenly, seemed to collect himself. "But I forget," he said with simple dignity. "You will wish to speak with the *capitán,* no doubt. But then you will be a guest in our home, tonight and for as long as you wish."

"Well, I don't—" Faver began, but the giant was already backing away into the crowd. Faver heard a quiet chuckle behind him and turned to see Captain Ordoñez standing at the door of his office.

"The sentry said a ghost was riding into the square." Ordoñez smiled, but his eyes moved over Faver's face, searching. "You're an awfully healthy-looking ghost. Did your mission go well?"

The confused happiness drained out of Faver at once as the memories came back. "You know I rescued Paco," he said. He lifted a hand to touch the ridged scar on his cheek. "But I didn't exactly get Nantahe. He got me."

"Yes, we know about Paco. You are a great hero here—to some of our people." The captain's tone suggested there were some who weren't so sure. He nodded toward the church. "There are candles burning for you there, and—well, you see."

Faver turned. The crowd had drawn away momentarily, but now it was back. A woman from the market, her head covered by a shawl, stepped forward. Without looking at Faver, she knelt and placed a frantically cackling chicken at his feet. She backed away and another took her place, to offer a folded blanket. A man in the tight trousers and vest of a *vaquero* unclasped a belt with a heavy silver buckle and added it to the growing pile.

Faver looked back at Ordoñez. "Captain, tell them to stop. I don't want—"

Ordoñez shook his head sharply. He stood almost at attention, and his thin face was stern.

Faver understood. These were proud people, as proud in their own way as the Apaches. They believed he had helped them, and they offered their gifts in gratitude. To refuse would shame them. They didn't know that he had gone after Paco for his own reasons, or that he himself had brought on much of their trouble.

He knew, though. He knew, as they came one after another, each leaving some token and shrugging off his words of thanks. The last was a little girl, eight or nine years old, with huge, frightened dark eyes. She smiled shyly and pressed a bunch of yellow wild flowers into his hand, then scurried away to hide her face in her mother's skirts.

"They trust you," Ordoñez said, so softly that the words didn't carry beyond Faver. After a moment, he added, "I hope they're right."

Faver turned to face him, tried to say something, gave up and shook his head. Nothing in his training, nothing in his life with the Apaches had prepared him for something like this. He wanted a chance to be by himself, to think things out, but there wasn't time right now.

"Faver," Braswell's voice said. The trader had come up while the villagers were still bringing their gifts. He pumped Faver's hand. "I'm glad to see you," he said, not looking especially glad. "We all thought they'd killed you out there."

Glad of the interruption, Faver grinned at him. "It was close," he said.

He was getting back on balance now. Of course, Braswell had known damn well he was alive all along. If Estella hadn't told him, Zamora surely had—but the trader could hardly explain that to Ordoñez.

"Your pardon." The captain's voice was gently ironic. "I don't wish to spoil your reunion, but perhaps you will take the time to tell me why you weren't killed. Come into my office, please. And you, Señor Braswell, if you wish."

Braswell wished, all right. Probably, Faver thought, the trader would have given a lot, like an arm and a couple of teeth, to know what he planned to tell Ordoñez.

"Captain?" He paused, looking back toward the heaped gifts. "Can you have your men take care of that?" There was just a little more bite in his voice than he'd intended. "They can put it in my old cell, if I'm going back there."

Ordoñez didn't smile. "I trust that won't be necessary. A moment."

He gave orders to one of his soldiers, then ushered Faver and Braswell into the office. Settling himself behind the desk, he nodded Faver to a chair.

"And now, your story?"

Faver reported briefly and accurately. He didn't mention his visit to the old woman, Juana, but otherwise he told the whole story of the search for the Apache hideout, Paco's escape, his own capture by Nantahe. He said very little about Chicuelo and Scar, or about his long crawl to reach the road. Part of that was nobody's business but his.

"A couple of peasants found me on the road and hauled me home with them," he finished. He saw Braswell, who had been listening intently and with growing signs of nervousness, relax and lean back in his chair. "Their farm was away out in the *barrancas,* and they didn't have any neighbors, so I was pretty well stuck there until I got back on my feet. Then I came here."

Ordoñez shook his head in wonder. "You were very lucky. Or perhaps it was more than luck." He thought a moment, then asked casually, "And these peasants, did they give you that fine horse and the rifle?"

"No, those belong to Mr. Braswell. His candelilla crew came through a couple of days ago. When I told them who I was, one of them loaned me his horse and gun, so I could get back to town." He looked innocently at the trader. "I want to be sure and thank him when he comes back."

Braswell's lips were tight. "Think nothing of it," he growled. "Glad to help."

"I see," Ordoñez said. "That explains it." Suddenly and surprisingly, he smiled. "But you have an invitation to the Guerrero home, and a hero's welcome. Tomorrow will be soon enough for planning. If I could see you in the morning, perhaps?"

"Sure, Captain. Whatever you say." Faver stood up and glanced at Braswell. "Say, about that rifle: Nantahe got mine, and I'm a little short on cash. Wonder if you could trust me?"

He knew he was pushing, and Braswell knew it, too. The trader laughed, but his eyes held cold murder.

"Keep it as a gift. You may need it, before you're through."

It was late in the morning before he got back to the Guardia office, and his head was none too clear even then. Valentín Guerrero had thrown quite a party.

"It's too bad Estella isn't here," Aunt Concepción had said. "She'll be so disappointed to miss your return."

If Estella hadn't been there, half the town had. Aunt Concepción and her women friends had cooked a huge supper. There had been guitars and dancing, and a great deal of highly potent mescal. More than enough, Faver thought.

The sentry beside the captain's door snapped up his rifle in a salute as Faver approached. Faver responded with a wave and went in without knocking. There should, he thought, be some advantages to being a hero.

Ordoñez had a military map of the area spread on his field desk. He looked up, nodded a greeting. For a disconcerting moment, Faver remembered his visit to Zamora's hut. He slid into a chair, rubbing a hand across his eyes, and waited for Ordoñez to say something.

"Buenas tardes," the captain said at last. He showed white teeth in a smile. "You slept well?"

"Reckon so. I really don't remember."

"I'm not surprised. I visited the celebration for a time, but I doubt you remember that, either."

"And I doubt you got me down here to talk about my drinking habits. I figured you'd heard from Mexico City, and they said to run me out of the country."

Ordoñez leaned back in his chair, drumming his fingers on the map. "As a matter of fact, I didn't get around to reporting your presence to Mexico City. It seemed better to wait." He frowned. "And you have made too many friends here for me to run you out of the country."

That wasn't a factor Faver would have expected to weigh heavily with the captain, but he said nothing. After a moment, Ordoñez turned his attention back to the map.

"I've been thinking about the Apache *ranchería*. Is this the way you saw it?"

Faver leaned over the map. The captain had penciled in the valley and the passages from the desert and the road.

"This big canyon starts out a little more to the south, about here. And it's narrower and more winding than you have it."

"Like this?" Carefully, Ordoñez made the changes. "If I brought the *tropa* through the desert by night, as you came, could I surprise the Indians?"

"Not a chance." Faver's voice held flat finality. "Three or four men could hold the pass into the valley against an army, and there are twenty good places for an ambush along the approaches. You'd be lucky to get half your men out alive."

"So. And the other entrance?"

"Even worse. Lots of places, that canyon's no more than thirty yard wide, and the Apaches would control the rim." He shrugged. "Even if you could force your way in, all you'd find would be an empty camp. The renegades could filter back into the hills any time you got too close."

"You don't paint an optimistic picture," Ordoñez said. "Very well. I wonder if you would tell me what you plan to do now."

"I have a horse and a rifle, and I figure I can get supplies. I'm going out after Nantahe and Chicuelo. And another one, called Scar."

This time, he would have no hesitation about killing from ambush. Nantahe was no longer his brother. There were no rules.

Ordoñez shook his head sadly.

"I thought so. Once, I would have welcomed that, but now it is too late. Killing them will not help."

Almost unconsciously, Faver touched the scar on his cheek. He looked at Ordoñez, but for a moment he saw only the night and the indifferent stars and his own blood sinking into the sand.

"It'll help me," he whispered. He shook himself. "The last time we talked, you wanted them dead."

"That was two months ago. Things have changed. Look here." Ordoñez leaned over the map, pointing with a stub of pencil. "The Apaches are everywhere. They run off stock here, murder a shepherd there, and vanish. We patrol, but it does no good and the people are frightened."

Faver nodded. That was the classic pattern of Apache warfare, the kind he'd seen so often before.

"Those are small raids," the captain went on. "A few men, a few shots fired. But in the last few weeks, things have changed."

With the pencil, he blocked out an area on the map, a broad rectangular stretch bordering on the desert Faver had crossed.

"Two small *ranchos* were attacked here, along the Bosque Largo. Everyone was killed. Then, the *hacienda* of Don Carlo Perez was raided, but his *vaqueros* beat the Apaches back. There were at least twenty in the party, Don Carlo says."

Interested in spite of himself, Faver studied the map. "Looks like they're trying to clear the area just east of their hideout," he said. "That would make it easier for them to move, and to watch the roads. It's the kind of thing Nantahe would do."

Ordoñez laughed bitterly. "He's doing it very well. You saw the people here in town, living in hovels, waiting for us to do something. But that isn't the worst. The Indians are drawing new recruits, getting stronger. They've tasted blood, and they'll be hard to stop."

"If Nantahe and Chicuelo were dead . . ." Faver began. His voice trailed off even before Ordoñez spoke.

"Yes?" the captain prompted. "What if they were?"

Faver didn't answer immediately. He knew what would happen as well as Ordoñez did. A new leader would come along, as Nana had come along to take over the remnant of Victorio's band after the great war chief was killed. The renegades had finally been run down, but the chase had been long and bloody.

"Before Nantahe came, these *broncos* in the hills were disorganized," Ordoñez said. "Now, they are a fighting force. They could be an army."

Faver pulled back suddenly, remembering. Nantahe. Chicuelo. Scar.

"I'm just interested in three of them. The rest aren't my problem."

"No?"

Ordoñez reached into a drawer, held something out to Faver. It was a belt, with intricately tooled leather and a massive silver buckle.

"I kept this for you. The rest has been taken to the Guerrero house." A hint of a smile. "My men, I regret to say, ate the chickens."

Holding the belt in his hands, Faver remembered not the gifts, the squash and blankets and wild flowers, but the people. The hard-faced *vaquero,* the little girl, the others in the crowd. Aunt Concepción, shyly proud to have him as a guest, and Paco, who'd slipped up to whisper to him the night before, "I knew you were alive, but Estella wouldn't let me tell. Thank you."

And Estella.

"The Apaches won't be careless again," Ordoñez said. "If you go out alone, they'll be waiting. They'll hear of you, and you will be one against twenty."

Faver hardly heard him. A stone fell into the water. Ripples spread away and rebounded, crossed and changed, until the man who had dropped the stone hardly recognized the pattern.

For a moment, Faver's resolve wavered. He hesitated, rubbing his chin thoughtfully, but his fingers touched the ridge of scar tissue on his cheek and the hatred rose in him again. He knew what he had to do, and nothing could change it.

"My men are good soldiers," Ordoñez was saying, "but they do not understand this kind of fighting. If you could scout for them, train them as Nantahe has trained his force, perhaps then we could strike back."

"Maybe you could."

There was good sense in what the captain said, Faver realized. Alone, he might find his way to Nantahe and the others, but he might equally well die along the way, his revenge not satisfied. Maybe the Guardia could give Nantahe and Chicuelo something to think about, something that would make his job easier. And if Ordoñez chose to believe he was helping out of a feeling of guilt, that was all right, too.

Abruptly, he stood up. Rolling the belt tightly around its buckle, he thrust it into his pocket.

"When do you want me to start?" he asked.

CHAPTER 14

Faver awoke instantly at the touch on his shoulder. From the angle of the sun and the shadows on the high bank of the gully in which he lay, he knew it was late afternoon. One of the Guardia soldiers, a stocky private whom everyone called Fito, was squatting beside him.

"What is it?"

"Dust, *señor*." The sentry's voice was barely a whisper. He held a pair of field glasses out to Faver. "Just a little puff, a feather."

"Stray cow, maybe. Or one of the cowhands."

"Or El Presidente Díaz, come to give us all a medal. But you'd better look."

"*Bueno.*"

Faver rolled to his feet, shrugging off the tattered blanket that covered him. For no good reason, he'd caught a touch of Fito's excitement. He'd had the patrol staked out here for four days, waiting. They were due for some luck.

A dozen yards upstream, the gully gnawed into the base of a rocky outcrop. The rocks rose a few feet above the surrounding plain, providing concealment and a wide view for a man who was careful. Faver snaked up the bank and stretched out flat, bringing the glasses to his eyes.

He looked first at the buildings a quarter-mile away. Bunkhouse, stables, cook shack—just a line camp on Don Carlo's vast ranch, but it guarded the best waterhole in the area. Sooner or later, Nantahe's bunch was sure to hit it. Faver hoped it would be soon.

He saw the smoke rising from the iron stovepipe, the unsaddled horses still in the corral. Then he shifted the glasses to sweep the surrounding country. The camp stood in a sea of waving yellow grass, broken here and there by low brown islands of rock. To the west, the grass ran out into desert, the desert Faver had crossed to reach Nantahe's *ranchería*. The setting sun hung just above the tall peak on the horizon.

Another chain of mountains rose abruptly a few miles to the east. The land between seemed to be flat and perfectly lifeless, but Faver knew that it was neither. The plain was laced with deep, narrow washes like the one where he and Fito were camped, half overgrown with grass and invisible until a rider was almost on top of them. In a larger gully three hundred yards to the northeast, a sergeant and eight troopers were camped—waiting, as Faver waited, for something to happen.

Gravel scraped, and Fito eased into position beside him. "There." The soldier's breath was warm against his ear. "Back to the west of north, where the big wash runs down into the desert."

Faver trained the glasses and waited. A minute passed, two, five. He felt his mind wandering, jerked it savagely back to the present. Ten. Twelve.

Then he felt Fito's body go rigid beside him. "There! *Dios mío*, it's them!"

He didn't need the warning—he'd seen it, too. Something big, man-big, darting across an open space just west of the line camp, vanishing again into the grass.

"It's them!" Fito repeated.

"Maybe." Faver sounded more doubtful than he felt. It all fit, the Apaches attacking at dusk, the sun at their backs. They would have the advantage of surprise, and the coming darkness would hide a retreat, should one be necessary.

There would be another surprise, if everything went right. Faver hoped the men of the patrol were ready. They weren't the best, but they were better than they'd been when he first agreed to help Ordoñez. "Your troops aren't good enough to tackle Nantahe," he'd told the captain bluntly. "They need training." A month had passed since then—a month of hard, grinding work.

Training they had gotten. Marksmanship, discipline, long rides on scant food and water—all had been part of the course. Constant patrolling of the back country had been seasoned with constant drill at the barracks. A few had deserted, but the men who stayed had developed a ragged sort of spirit that held them together. They were close to being soldiers.

"That's the best we can do," Faver had said the week before. "Now, we need Apaches."

Ordoñez was somewhere off to the south with a dozen men, watching a *hacienda* that had beaten off an earlier attack. Most of the remaining troopers, under Sergeant Noh, were carrying on patrols as usual. Faver had chosen to watch the line camp.

"The dust again. Look."

Fito was right. Just by the head of the wash was a swirl of dust, instantly carried away by the wind. For a long minute, there was nothing more. Then an Apache, on foot and crouching low, slipped over the edge of the draw and out onto the plain.

Through the glasses, Faver could see him quite clearly, a hard-faced warrior with a green headcloth. He wasn't one of the bunch who'd been with Nantahe, but that didn't mean much. He found cover beside a clump of cactus and waited. Soon, a second Apache, probably the scout Faver had seen earlier, crawled back to join him.

"This is it," Faver whispered without looking away. "Fito, get the horses. Check everything, and tighten the cinches. Be ready to move."

Fito slipped away with an agility surprising for a man with his build. Out on the flats, the first Apache motioned with his hand, and three others emerged from the draw to disappear into the tall grass. Another gesture brought three more, and soon there were twelve, including the leader and the scout. They worked swiftly toward the line camp, three or four dashing forward at a time, while the others covered them.

Nantahe had been doing some training, too, Faver thought grimly. Putting the glasses aside, he drew a fragment of mirror from his shirt pocket.

The Apaches were barely fifty yards from the bunkhouse, still unseen by the *vaqueros* there, when Faver caught the last rays of the sun and flashed a signal to the draw where his patrol waited. Nothing happened. Two Indians moved, then dropped prone in the grass while the others came up.

Come on, Faver thought, almost aloud. Fuentes, a skinny noncom who'd stood guard at the jail, was in charge over there. Totally against Faver's expectations, the man had proved to be an excellent squad leader. Ordoñez had made him a sergeant, but he hadn't been tried in battle. He might be asleep, or drunk, or he might have decided not to fight today.

The raiders were coming into line now. Faver drew his pistol. A shot might warn the *vaqueros,* but he knew it was too late, knew the Apaches' first volley would catch them unaware. Sickness rising in him, he saw the leader straighten and raise his arm to give the signal.

Mounted troopers exploded out of the gully to the northeast, horses lurching up the steep bank and plunging into a gallop on the plain. Fuentes rode in the lead, leaning low on his pony's neck, his right arm out rigid and a pistol in his hand. The soldiers fanned out left and right into a ragged line, pounding wildly down toward the startled Apaches.

Faver heard the crack of carbines and the deeper-toned bark of answering fire. A trooper spun from the saddle, but two of the Indians were already down in the grass. Without waiting to see more, Faver was up and running, concealment forgotten. He slid down into the gully. Fito was waiting, mounted and holding the reins of Faver's buckskin.

"The big dry wash!" Faver snatched the reins and swung into the saddle, pulling the horse around. "They left their horses there. We can cut them off!"

He spurred up out of the gully and drove across the open ground, Fito at his shoulder. The flank of the raiders had swept past, and the two of them were behind the main group. Now they were closer to the wash than the Apaches, and coming in at a different angle.

He swerved to miss the head of a gully, a nasty yard-deep slash in the prairie. Warned by his move, Fito jumped his mount across it and took the lead. A wide draw leading down toward the main channel opened out on their right, and Fito reined his horse into it without hesitation.

"They'll have guards!" Faver yelled. "Look out!"

Fito turned his head for an instant, his teeth gleaming white in a grin. He drew his pistol and spurred on unchecked.

Faver jerked the Marlin out of its boot—he wouldn't use the awkward across-the-back sling the Mexicans favored—and levered a shell into the chamber, guiding his horse with his knees. He was three lengths behind Fito when the soldier rounded a bend and burst out onto the floor of the dry wash.

There were three Apaches there, two of them trying to contain fifteen plunging ponies. The third, crouched below the lip of the gully, fired his rifle methodically to cover the retreat of the raiding party. Fito's horse plunged almost into the middle of the Apache herd. The Indian ponies gave way, two or three of them breaking free to bolt down the wash into the desert beyond.

The trooper fired twice from his rearing mount, his second bullet knocking down one of the horse-holders. The other dropped the halters and ran, cutting toward Fito and ducking almost under the neck of his horse. Fito reined back hard and swung his arm across to line up the pistol. Before he could squeeze the trigger, the man on the cutbank turned and fired at him.

It all happened in a moment. Faver, barreling around the bend in Fito's wake, saw the troop horse go up on its back legs, stagger, crash down sideways. Flung headlong into the rocky floor of the gully, Fito hit hard and lay still. Faver pulled up so short that the buckskin almost fell. He twisted in the saddle, reins forgotten, swinging his rifle up and around.

He caught a blurred glimpse of the warrior—blue breechclout and coppery skin, hands busy reloading a single-shot carbine. He levered off three shots and saw sand kick up around the Indian. Then the Apache was gone and Faver was off his horse, stumbling to one knee and lurching up in pursuit.

He never knew what stopped him—a movement seen from the corner of his eye, or some instinct for danger, or only the belated realization that one renegade was still unaccounted for. Whatever the reason, he stopped and spun around just as the surviving horse-holder snatched up Fito's fallen pistol.

The Indian struggled to cock the unfamiliar weapon. As he brought it up with both hands locked around the butt, Faver shot him.

He aimed low, hoping to get a prisoner, but the bullet lacked the shattering force of the Springfield's massive slug. It knocked the Apache's leg out from under him and tumbled him on the ground beside Fito, but the Indian held onto the pistol. Still full of fight, he rolled, thrusting the weapon out in front of him and jerking at the trigger.

The shot went wild. Faver rapped off two rounds from the rifle and saw the impact of the bullets flatten the warrior in the dust. He came forward carefully, kicked the revolver away from the motionless hand, then knelt for a moment over the body. No prisoner this time.

Beyond the banks of the wash, the firing had died away to an occasional flurry. The shots seemed to be centered off in the southwest now. The third Apache had disappeared completely. He and the other raiders who had survived Fuentes' charge would be falling back into the desert, sheltered by the coming night. Already the sun was below the horizon. Anyone the patrol hadn't caught by now, they probably weren't going to get.

Faver stooped over the Apache Fito had shot, then straightened quickly. The man had been hit in the face. There was no doubt he was dead. Lowering the rifle's hammer to half-cock, Faver knelt beside Fito.

There was blood on the trooper's head, oozing from an ugly gash in his scalp. Below that was an egg-shaped lump, but no sign of a bullet wound.

It took Faver a minute to figure out what had happened. The Apache's snap shot had missed Fito, passing within inches as he turned in the saddle. It had smashed into the back of the troop horse's head, killing the animal instantly. Fito had managed to clear the saddle when he fell, but he hadn't had much choice in his landing. He was unconscious and one leg seemed to be broken, but he was breathing strongly and was very much alive.

Faver sat back on his heels, surprised at his feeling of relief, at the depth of affection he'd developed for the stocky trooper. He was going to have to watch himself. That was more emotion than a good Apache would show and, until this was over, he had to be a better Apache than Nantahe.

Footsteps crunched on the rim of the gully. He turned, bringing up the rifle, hammer thumbed back. Then he grinned and lowered the gun. Fuentes stood there, dark against the sky, his big smile visible even in the twilight. Three troopers flanked him, all looking down at the scene in the gully.

"We did it! We killed four, maybe more, of their rear guard. The others scattered, and we hunted them into the desert!"

"That's good. Did you get the leader, the big one with the green headband?"

"¿Quién sabe? We'll find out in the morning. Two of my men were wounded, and one of the vaqueros who joined in was killed. But the men were heroes, all of them!"

"Yeah." The excitement of combat was draining out of Faver, leaving him tired and empty. "You'd better call the rest in, before they scatter too far. And get a lantern from the line camp. We have another wounded hero down here."

The troopers weren't used to being victorious. Word had somehow spread that they were coming in, complete with battle trophies and wounded. Half the town had turned out to meet them, with the peasants who'd been driven from their homes in the forefront. The surprised soldiers were greeted with cheers and shouted vivas. Fito and the other wounded men, sitting up in a borrowed wagon, were deluged with suggested remedies, kisses from the young girls, and offers by some of the older women that brought laughter from the crowd.

Fuentes tried briefly to keep order, then rolled his eyes at Faver and gave it up. Faver shrugged. A little dose of pride wouldn't hurt the troopers. They deserved their celebration. A search of the plain that morning before they pulled out had turned up four dead Apaches. The two killed in the gully made six, and he'd found bloodstains hinting that others had been wounded. The survivors would have to report failure with heavy losses to Nantahe. Faver didn't envy them.

Even so, he wasn't satisfied. They had hit the cut-offs and hurt them. That was good, but next time the Apaches would be more careful, stronger, better armed. General Miles had needed five thousand men to dig Geronimo and his hundred warriors out of hiding, and it had been the scouts—like Nantahe—who'd finally done the job. Ordoñez had barely fifty soldiers at his command.

Nantahe could afford to wait. Faver couldn't.

"Jess! Jess, wait!"

He was trying to ease away from the celebration, leading his horse back toward the stables. He hadn't seen Estella in the crowd, but he heard her cry above the babble of voices as he reached the edge of the square. He turned and her arms were suddenly around his neck.

"You're not hurt? We heard of the battle, but—"

"I'm all right," Faver interrupted gently, uncomfortably aware of his bristly beard, his week of ingrained trail dirt. "Look out. Think of your reputation."

She pressed against him more tightly, exclaiming, "I don't care!" but she did move away then, with a quick, guilty glance toward the crowd.

"It's good to see you," Faver said, honestly enough. There hadn't been much chance to talk with her during the past month, between the patrolling and the process of pulling the Guardia into shape. And, of course, there was Ordoñez. "I figured Braswell would have you working today."

She looked away for a moment, and the smile slipped from her face. "No," she said. Then, before Faver could wonder about it, she raised her eyes to his again. "The one you seek—Nantahe—he wasn't there?"

Faver shook his head, his own face hardening. He'd never quite regained the weight he'd lost after being hurt. His face was thinner, and there was a grimness about his mouth and his jutting cheekbones.

"I was afraid you'd find him," she said. "Then you'd have no reason to stay."

"Not this time."

The buckskin neighed and tossed its head, yanking on the reins. Faver shook himself and grinned at the girl.

"Look, I have to take care of him. And I guess a bath and a shave wouldn't hurt me any. I'll see you later, at your aunt's house. All right?"

"Yes." There was something in her face he couldn't read, something only glimpsed there as she turned away. "Yes, I'll see you then."

He dined that night with the Guerreros, making polite conversation with Estella's uncle and Tía Concepción, answering questions from Paco and the other children—there seemed to be a houseful—about the ambush. After the meal, when talk began to drag, he smiled at Estella.

"I think I'll walk around the plaza to settle that good food. Would you like to come?" He nodded to Valentín Guerrero, adding, "With your permission, *señor*."

Tía Concepción frowned, turned away with a theatrical sigh. It was a difficult situation for her, Faver supposed. As Paco's rescuer, he was a saint, probably sent directly by the blessed *Virgen*. As the man who went walking with Estella after dark, he was a stray *gringo* who couldn't be trusted.

Estella threw a shawl about her shoulders and came to the door. Together, a proper distance apart, they walked up the dusty street. As they came within sight of the plaza, Faver saw there was still a crowd, soldiers and townsmen mixed together, milling before the Guardia barracks in the uncertain light of lanterns. He stopped.

"Must still be celebrating over there. Maybe I'd better take you back."

Estella looked back to the left, toward a narrow track that led uphill behind the town.

"We could go that way," she suggested. "A little higher up, you can look down on the town and all the valley. Luis and I—" She broke off abruptly, then finished, "I go there often."

Faver took her arm and turned up the trail. "Ordoñez should be back tomorrow morning," he said. "We sent a galloper to tell him the news. He'll probably call off the watch on Don Carlo's ranch for now."

"For now," she repeated. For a moment, she pulled a little away from him. Then she moved close again, leaned her head against his shoulder.

Neither spoke for the next few minutes. The trail slanted across the face of the hill, widened out into a flat, open space just below the crest. There was a little adobe shrine there, protecting the plaster statue of some saint. Beyond, the hillside fell away sharply, and Faver could see the town, huddled white below them in the moonlight.

Estella stopped there and turned to face him.

"And will that make such a difference, when Luis is here?"

Her tone was light, teasing, though her smile didn't quite match her words. Faver answered in kind.

"Some difference. I doubt he'd approve of us walking in the moonlight. I'll ask him, when this is over."

"How long is that, Jess?"

He shrugged. "As long as it takes. Until the cut-offs aren't a threat anymore." Then, almost to himself, "Until Nantahe and Chicuelo—"

He didn't finish, but Estella pulled back. She turned to look down toward the town, crossing her arms, hugging herself as if she were cold. "Maybe you were right. Maybe we should go back."

"'Stella?" She didn't look at him. He stepped up behind her, put his hands on her shoulders. "Something's been wrong all night. What's the matter?"

"Nothing. Nothing that you should worry about."

"Try me."

"It's—" She hesitated, then shook her head. "It's about Zamora and his men. They—"

"They don't blame you because I got away? Look, if they've tried to hurt you—"

She laughed, a little bit mockingly. "Oh, no one would hurt me. As Zamora said, who would expect a woman to act sensibly in such matters." There was a trace of bitterness in her voice, but only a trace. "But the bandits no longer trust me. Señor Braswell says I can't work for him anymore."

Faver laughed in relief. "Is that all? You had me worried for a minute."

Her body stiffened under his hands. "It's important to me," she said. "I told you what that job meant. But it doesn't matter to you. Nothing matters except your revenge, except killing."

He tightened his grip on her, hardly aware that his fingers were digging into her flesh. When he finally spoke, the words came raggedly, one at a time. "You know what they did to me."

"Yes. But I don't think you do." Now she turned, close against him, looking up into his face. "You don't care about us—not me, or Luis, or any of the people here. We're only—only tools, something to use to help you find Nantahe."

"'Stella." She tried to pull away from him, striking out angrily when he held on. "It isn't like that, 'Stella. Wait."

He caught her in a sort of bear hug, pinioning her arms, drawing her closer. He'd intended only to hold her until her anger cooled, to explain somehow how he felt, but the touch of her body awoke the sleeping hunger in him. He bent his head, captured her mouth with his. For a moment longer she struggled. Then her body relaxed against his, her hands reached to clutch at his back.

"Perhaps I am interrupting?"

The captain's voice was dead level and very soft. Faver and Estella broke apart, staring at him. He stood at the top of the trail, a few paces away. In the fitful moonlight, his face was unreadable.

"Luis—" the girl began.

"I looked for you in your quarters, then at the Guerreros'," he cut in, still quietly, speaking to Faver. "They said you were walking." He glanced at Estella, then away. "I thought perhaps you'd come here."

Estella took a step back, shook off Faver's hand. She looked at him for a moment, her face almost as cold as the captain's. Then she turned, brushing past Ordoñez, and walked quickly back down the trail toward La Morita.

Faver took a half-step after her, stopped. "It's my fault, *compadre*," he said, facing Ordoñez. "Not hers."

"Perhaps." Ordoñez might have smiled. "I suppose I should kill you. It's expected." He waved a hand, dismissing it. "We will talk of that later. It is not why I forced our march back here."

A sudden coldness gripped Faver. "What happened?"

"Your messenger reached us just before noon, and we planned to march home tomorrow. Then, just at dark, we had another report."

He paused, but Faver didn't speak. After a moment, he continued. "A *vaquero* from the line camp stumbled in. He'd been wounded, and his horse gave out on the way, but he was the lucky one."

Faver closed his eyes. "Nantahe." It wasn't a question. He knew.

"The Apaches hit the line camp again, late this afternoon. The *vaqueros* might have been drunk, and there was no warning. They killed all but the one."

CHAPTER 15

The sentry on guard outside the barracks that morning had been in the fight at the line camp. He seemed to hold himself a little straighter than before, with a hint of pride in the set of his shoulders. If his brown linen uniform was as slovenly as ever, his carbine was clean and newly oiled.

Captain Ordoñez and Sergeant Fuentes were down at the stables, he told Faver. The captain's compliments, and would Señor Faver join them there at once?

Reluctantly, Faver went. He'd really messed things up the night before, with both Estella and Ordoñez. He didn't know what the captain might have decided overnight, but it probably wouldn't be good. He might have ruined his best chance to get at Nantahe. For the first time, he wondered if that was the most important thing.

"Buenos días," Ordoñez greeted him. "We've been waiting for you."

The gear and clothing taken from the dead Apaches had been spread on a blanket in the wagon yard. Fuentes was kneeling, turning a short, horn-backed bow in his hands while a couple of troopers on morning stable duty watched surreptitiously. Ordoñez stood nearby. If Faver had been wondering how he would react, the captain's set face gave him no help. Outwardly, Ordoñez wasn't reacting at all.

"Sergeant Fuentes has given me a full report on the combat. That, at least, was satisfactory."

"The troop did well," Faver replied. "Sergeant Fuentes especially. We must have hurt the Apaches badly, for Nantahe to think he had to hit back so fast."

Fuentes looked up at him, surprise and pleasure mingled on his face. Ordoñez didn't answer directly. Instead, he gestured to the items piled on the blanket.

"Perhaps you can learn something from this."

Faver stooped to look. It wasn't much of a haul: a checked cotton shirt and a rawhide vest, both bloodstained; other bits of clothing; moccasins—newly made from cowhide, not deer or antelope; a worn hunting knife; a dozen other things.

"This is a wicked-looking thing." Fuentes took an arrow from a beaded quiver, nocked it to the bowstring. "One of the Apaches shot an arrow at me. But it's no match for a pistol."

Faver grinned. "You're lucky he didn't put it through your gizzard. Here."

He took the bow, looked for a target. There was a watering trough across the stable yard, thirty yards away.

"See the knot in that plank? Right there."

He bent the bow as he spoke, feathered tip of the arrow back to his ear, fingers opening with the relaxed ease Nantahe had been so long in teaching him. The bowstring sang, drawing blood from his unprotected wrist. There was a solid thwack, and the arrow quivered in the plank an inch or two from the knot. Ordoñez raised his eyebrows.

"I'm not very good," Faver apologized. He handed back the bow. "The Apache was probably better. If he'd been smart enough to shoot at your horse instead of you, he could have caused you some trouble."

"Maybe. If I waited until he was close enough."

"Some of the clothing came from the Alvarado raid, we think," Ordoñez said. "And we found an old shotgun that belonged to another farmer." He paused, then went on thoughtfully. "Only one more gun was captured—a lever-action rifle much like yours, Señor Faver. How many of the others had guns?"

Fuentes straightened. "Most of the raiding party, I'm sure. Private Solis was shot in the shoulder, and three of our horses were hit. The rifle belonged to one of the Apache rear guard."

"One of the three in the gully had a military carbine of some kind," Faver put in. "I don't know about the horse-holders. One of them tried for Fito's pistol."

"Even so, they don't seem to be well armed. Are you sure we can't attack their camp?"

"Dead sure." Faver rubbed his wrist absently. "You might beat the hostiles in a stand-up fight, but that isn't what you'd get. We've talked about it already."

Ordoñez made an impatient gesture. "But what we've done so far hasn't helped. Would you have us go on patrolling as we have been? It plays into the Apaches' hands."

"You're right."

Momentarily taken aback at such ready agreement, Ordoñez said nothing. Faver searched for words. He turned through the clothing on the blanket, hardly seeing it, picturing the way Nantahe would run his campaign.

"We ought to have the jump on the hostiles, but we don't. I figured one good whipping, and that bunch of *broncos* would start to come apart. Nantahe thought so, too, but he was smart enough to do something about it."

"You couldn't have known—"

"I'm supposed to know. Now, we're back where we started. The Apaches will be more careful, but they'll keep raiding. They'll get guns, finally—steal enough, or find someplace they can trade for them. If they know I'm alive—and they may, that Indian in the wash saw me—they'll move their camp to a place where nobody can find it."

Ordoñez squatted beside him, frowning. "You don't paint a pretty picture."

"It gets worse. There are plenty of young Apache braves back in the hills who'll join Nantahe if they think he's winning. I doubt he has more than thirty warriors now, and you have to stop him before he gets stronger. You'll have to patrol, keep him moving, set up garrison posts at the key waterholes. Can you get more men? Regulars, maybe, from the central government?"

Fuentes muttered something and spat on the ground. Ordoñez glanced at him, came back to Faver.

"As you see, it wouldn't be a popular idea. The *regulares* are drafted men, convicts, the worst sort of scum. They would be quartered here and on the other villages, and their officers would take charge of the campaign." He shrugged. "Almost, I would rather have the Apaches."

"Well, you've got them. We'll have to manage the best we can, maybe borrow some *vaqueros* from the big ranches. We can slow the hostiles down, hurt them some. But we can't beat them. Not unless we're awfully lucky."

"Maybe they will come out and fight," Fuentes offered. "You tricked them once, with the ambush. There must be a way to do it again."

"It won't be—" Faver began. Then his voice died away. He stared down at the long strip of cloth he'd picked up from the heap on the blanket. "Where did this come from?"

"What?" Fuentes reached out for it, but Faver didn't let go. "Oh, that was the headcloth their leader wore. You know, the big one you asked about. We found him dead down near the line camp."

Faver nodded, but he barely heard. A lot of things he'd noticed, minor things, seemed to be pulling themselves into a pattern now. If he was right, the pattern had a mighty interesting shape to it.

"How bad do you want to nail the renegades, Captain? Enough to take some chances?"

"Enough to answer foolish questions," Ordoñez snapped. Then, more softly, "Enough to do whatever I must. Even to call in the *regulares,* if there's no other way." He frowned. "What is it? Do you have a plan?"

"An idea, maybe." Carefully, Faver folded the headband flat and tucked it into his pocket. "Give me until tomorrow, *amigo.* Maybe I can work something out."

The storeroom of Braswell's place smelled of new harness and saddle soap, overlain with the stink of kerosene and the heavy, musty odor of the baled candelilla. It was almost totally dark, the only light being a pale yellow gleam that showed through the crack under the door.

Faver had slipped inside while Braswell was busy in his office and the new clerk was occupied with customers. He'd learned what he wanted to know almost at once, and now he needed to have a talk with Braswell, alone and without interruptions.

He heard the slam of the big front door, the rattling of chains and bolts as it was locked for the night. Gliding across the room, he placed his ear against the storeroom door. He heard voices, Braswell's deep laugh carrying over the others.

"—wouldn't say that." The trader was coming closer, at least one other man with him. "Anyway, we need to move those cases down from the loft. Don Carlo's men will be here to get them in the morning, and he doesn't like to be kept waiting."

A second voice offered a suggestion as to where Don Carlo could put his supplies, and a third embellished it. Braswell and two of his hired hands, then. Faver retreated behind a pile of flour sacks in a dark corner, made himself comfortable. It was still too early to move.

Perhaps two hours passed before he eased the door open and peered outside. Braswell's two helpers had left by the back door some time before, and the trader's footsteps had gone past the storeroom and faded into silence. Faver gave him a little time to get settled, then stepped out into the darkened store. Braswell had a couple of rooms upstairs, but there was still a light in the office. Faver approached carefully.

It was a big room, with a heavy iron safe in one corner. There were no windows, but the walls were hung with bright-colored blankets and serapes. An oil lamp provided light, and a low fire burned in the potbellied stove.

Braswell sat with his back to the door, bending over his big, polished, dark desk. He was making entries in a battered ledger. A shotgun leaned against the wall to his right, a handy arm's-length away.

"Don't reach for it," Faver said conversationally. "I just want to visit for a while."

The trader started violently, but he made no move toward the gun. After a moment, he picked up a blotter, methodically dabbed up spilled ink, and finished the line he'd been writing. Then he snapped the book closed and laid it on the desk.

"Goddamn you and your Apache tricks, Faver." He didn't turn around, but he sounded more annoyed than frightened. "The store's closed. What do you want?"

"Help. You're going to give it to me. You and I are going to set a trap for Nantahe."

Now Braswell did turn around, staring at Faver in undisguised astonishment.

"You're crazy. I thought so all along, and now I'm sure. Get out of here, before I—"

"Before you what? Your men are gone for the night. You could holler for the soldiers, but you probably don't want the captain to know I saw your wagon in Zamora's camp."

"So. This is some kind of badger game."

Braswell leaned back in his chair, gazing thoughtfully at Faver. He stroked his beard with one hand. The other swung down by his side casually, moved toward the shotgun.

"Don't." Faver touched his holstered pistol. It was a double-action weapon of the type the Guardia used. He didn't like it much, but it was menacing enough. "I don't want to kill you, but you don't have to be in perfect health. Move away."

The trader moved, watching Faver warily. There still was no fear in his eyes. He was getting back on balance, beginning to think again. That was fine. The more clearly Braswell was thinking, the better.

"You might as well sit down, Faver." He opened his coat with exaggerated care, took out a cigar. "Put the gun over there, if it worries you. You just startled me, that's all."

Faver perched on the edge of the desk. Braswell returned to his chair, settled back. He lit his cigar and took a puff.

"You know, I don't think you'll say anything to Ordoñez about the bandits. It would be your word against mine, and mine's plenty good with the *jefe político* here." He paused and chuckled. "And it would surely raise a lot of questions about 'Stella. I hear you're not doing too well with her as it is."

Faver set his teeth together, managed a smile. "Reckon you're right. I can't prove you're working with Zamora." He reached into his pocket, took out the folded headband. "But then, I don't have to prove it. I have this."

"What—?" Braswell squinted at the cloth as Faver spread it on the desk. In the soft lamplight, the design of fine gold threads showed clearly against the green cloth. "I don't see—"

"This is sure a popular pattern," Faver interrupted quietly. "An Apache the troops killed was wearing this. One of Zamora's girls was making a dress out of some material just like it." He paused, watching Braswell's face. "And there's another bolt of it back in your storeroom, right now."

Beads of sweat had suddenly appeared on the trader's forehead. He stared at the strip of cloth, reached out for it with dreamlike slowness. Faver waited until his fingers touched it, then slapped the hand aside and shoved him back into his chair.

"You're playing all three sides." His voice was cold and level, riding over Braswell's mumbled protests. "You trade with Zamora for stolen stock, and you're doing the same with the Apaches. Then you're playing respectable citizen here." He grabbed the front of Braswell's shirt, jerked him upright. "How many guns have you run to Nantahe? How many?"

"No—none. Not guns. No."

Faver pushed him away in disgust. "I don't need to turn you over to the soldiers. Suppose Zamora found out you were dealing with the hostiles? Or the farmers out there—they wouldn't ask for proof." He paused to let Braswell think about that, then leaned close to him. "I could even get word to Nantahe that you're double-crossing him. Want me to tell you what the Apaches do to traitors?"

"No, you couldn't do that. Nobody could. Listen, Faver—"

"Try me."

"—We can make a deal. There's money in this business. I could cut you in."

"You'll do better than that," Faver said. Braswell started to speak, but Faver cut him off, his voice snapping like a whip. "Shut up and listen! You can try to talk your way out of this, but I don't think Nantahe or Zamora will listen. You can try to run—and I know a damn good scout who'll help track you down. Or you can play it straight with me. You're a smart man. You decide. Now."

There was a long silence, broken only by the trader's heavy breathing. Faver waited, hand resting on the butt of his pistol. Braswell might still try to make a break, but he didn't expect it. The man had cracked.

Finally, Braswell bowed his head, rubbed one hand across his eyes. His face was pale above the bristling beard, and he spoke almost too softly for Faver to hear.

"No guns, Faver. Not that. I never gave them guns, I swear."

"That must've been hard to manage. Nantahe wanted guns, didn't he?"

"Nantahe! He isn't human!" Braswell raised his head suddenly, stared at Faver. "Ordoñez told me you were his friend."

"Once." Faver almost reached to touch the scar on his jaw. He caught the impulse, let his hand fall back. "Once. How'd you get mixed up with him?"

"No trick to it. My boys—the candelilla pickers—know a lot of Apaches back in the hills. One of the bucks came to them, asked if we could buy some cattle. Of course, I didn't know where they came from—"

"Of course."

"—so I sold them to some friends of mine across the border. I gave the Apaches food, some other goods—that cloth you saw, I guess, tobacco, things like that."

"But they wanted more."

Braswell mopped his forehead. He straightened suddenly in the chair—so suddenly that Faver almost pulled his gun—and bent to open the bottom drawer of the desk. He took out a half-empty whiskey bottle and a glass.

"There's other glasses in the cupboard, if you want a drink. No?"

He poured a generous shot, downed it, and poured another.

"When did you see Nantahe?" Faver asked, when it seemed that Braswell wouldn't speak again.

"It was right after that first time." Braswell lifted the glass, then looked at it and set it down without drinking. "The Indian who set up the deal—Bonito, his name is—sent word he wanted to see me. I met him at a place down south of here. There were two others with him, Nantahe and the other one. Older, and with eyes like a snake."

"That'd be Chicuelo."

"I guess. Anyway, they wanted guns. I told them it was too risky, but—" He hesitated, then shrugged. "But they knew I'd dealt with Zamora."

The trader stopped, staring at the desk top. Almost, Faver felt a bit of sympathy for him. Braswell had been pulled in over his head, and he was in a bad position. Whatever he was remembering now, chances were it wasn't pleasant—but, unlike so many of the people who'd suffered from the Apaches, Braswell had asked for his trouble.

"They insisted," the trader finally said. "I've managed to stall them since then, and they've left my shipments alone. But lately—"

"I'd guess your time's running out."

"They stopped the candelilla wagon last week and took the driver's rifle. Didn't hurt anybody, but I figure it was a warning."

Braswell stared moodily at the polished wood. The fear in his eyes was fading, replaced with resignation, or maybe even relief.

"I'm between a rock and a hard place, Faver. I can't stall them any longer. They'll shut me down, or worse, unless I come up with guns." He looked up at Faver, nodded grimly. "And now I have you."

Faver grinned. "Don't worry. I'm going to help you, and the Apaches, too. How long would it take you to set up a shipment of rifles to Zamora's bunch?"

"Well—" Braswell hesitated, suddenly wary again. "I don't know. I'd have to talk to some people, make arrangements across the border." He pointed a finger at Faver. "If this is some kind of trick—"

"I don't need tricks. One word from me, and your friends will feed you to the coyotes." He waited, but the trader didn't speak. "Listen, after that fight with the Guardia, the Apaches will really be howling for guns. You'd better decide which side you're on, right now."

"Okay. It'll take two weeks. Maybe less, with money down. That'll be good for a couple of cases of rifles with ammunition."

"Fine. Then, there's just one more thing. I want you to set me up a meeting with Zamora."

The trader's mouth dropped open. "I was right. You really are crazy. Zamora will kill you on sight."

"Well, that should make you happy. Do it."

Braswell shook his head doubtfully. "I'll need some time. I'll let you know." Then, with a trace of his old shrewdness, "Seems funny, though, that you're trusting me this far. Like you said, you're the only one who knows about this."

Faver's lips skinned back in a grin that was more of a snarl.

"We need each other. Without me, you'll still have Nantahe to deal with, until he gets what he wants. I figure you're smart enough to see that."

"Well—" Braswell began. Faver held up his hand.

"Just in case you aren't, let me give you some advice. You'd better kill me first try. If I find out you've crossed me, you'll wish I'd turned you over to Nantahe."

The trader stared into his grim face. "My God," he said. "You're one of them. I'd heard you were more Apache than white." Then he blinked, another thought occurring to him. "Hey, it'll take money to get those guns, big money. Who's going to pay for them?"

This time, Faver's grin was real. "You guess," he said.

"Oh, no," Braswell croaked.

"If you don't like it, you can try to get a better deal from Nantahe, or Zamora. I don't mind."

"You son of a bitch." Braswell shook his head, a tone almost of admiration in his voice. He smiled wryly. "If you're still alive when this is over, look me up. You'd make a hell of a horse trader."

CHAPTER 16

"I don't think they're coming," Ordoñez said. He looked away from the window, frowned at Faver. "It's almost sundown. How much longer are we to wait for this"—he searched for a word, failed to find one that suited him—"for Zamora?"

"He'll come," Faver said. "Some of his men were along the road as we rode in. He's afraid of an ambush, and he's not much happier about this than you are. But he'll be here." If only to kill us, Faver added mentally, but there wasn't much point in saying it aloud. He'd had enough trouble talking Ordoñez into agreeing to meet with the bandit chieftain. Selling the idea to Zamora had been even harder. In the end, Zamora had insisted on naming the time and place, had required that Faver and Ordoñez leave their Guardia escort on the road and come the last two miles alone.

It added up to a perfect setup for a trap. If Faver had misjudged the bandit's intentions, he probably wouldn't have much time to regret the mistake.

"Some of his men?" Ordoñez demanded. He glared suspiciously over his shoulder. "Those *peones* with the oxcart? How do you know?"

"I recognized them." Faver saw the next question coming and tried to head it off. "I expect they're still back on the road, watching your men to see there's no funny business. The rest of the gang is probably outside, watching us."

Ordoñez returned his attention to the window without answering, for which Faver was silently grateful. He didn't know if it was chance or Zamora's sense of humor that had caused the bandit to choose, for the meeting, the abandoned *rancho* where Faver and Estella had spent the night of their escape. Whatever the reason, Ordoñez could have asked a number of questions that Faver would prefer not to answer.

"The light is gone." Ordoñez banged the crude wooden shutters closed. "Everything out there seems to be moving."

He strode across the room, turned and paced its length again. After a few more rounds, he dropped onto a bench and rested his elbows on the plank table.

"Maybe you'd better light the candle," Faver suggested. "They'll think something's wrong if we're waiting for them in the dark."

Ordoñez swore under his breath. He scratched a match across the tabletop and held it to the guttered candle. Squatting on his heels against the wall, Faver looked at him sympathetically. The captain was nervous, and with good reason.

They sat in silence for perhaps five minutes. Then Faver raised his head.

"They're here."

"What?" Ordoñez had been staring at the candle flame, lost in some thought of his own. "Where? I didn't hear anything."

"Two of them, maybe more. They've been prowling around outside for a couple of minutes, and I think they're about ready to come in." He coughed apologetically. "You might not want to make any sudden moves."

"Take care of yourself, *amigo*," Ordoñez snapped.

There was an emphasis on the last word that Faver didn't like at all, but before he had time to think about it, Zamora's men arrived.

A heavy step sounded just outside, and a booted foot smashed into the flimsy door. It slammed back. Two men came through fast, guns drawn, and took positions on either side of the doorway. Faver recognized Zamora's two bodyguards.

"Hands up! Don't move." That was the one who'd been assigned to follow him, back at Zamora's camp. "You, *gringo*, on your feet. Rabbit, get his gun."

The second bandit edged forward, keeping out of his comrade's line of fire. He stretched out a scrawny arm, yanked Faver's pistol from its holster. Then he backed carefully away, showing buck teeth in a grin.

"Now the *capitán*'s. He won't be needing it."

Ordoñez shot Faver a quick look, but he endured Rabbit's

fumbling stoically. The bandit finally got the holster flap open and withdrew the heavy pistol.

"*Bueno,* Javier. Do we shoot them now?"

Faver slid back down to his squatting position against the wall. He reached down casually and scratched his lower leg, his eyes on the one called Javier.

"Not yet. The *jefe* wants to see them first. Then we'll shoot them." His pistol jerked suddenly toward Faver. "Nobody told you to sit down. Our *jefe* is coming, see. Stand up."

Ordoñez snorted and dropped back onto the bench. The bandit turned on him, disbelief giving way to rage on his face. Faver tensed, but then another figure pushed through the shattered door.

"That's enough. Javier, Rabbit, put those guns away."

Zamora had dressed in his best to meet his old enemy. He wore a clean white shirt, with black vest and trousers that seemed to be molded to his skinny frame. A flowing green neckerchief at his throat and a gold sombrero dangling behind his shoulders completed the costume. Besides his gunbelt, he wore an Army-issue Mills belt filled with ammunition. He smiled, his flat and empty eyes resting on Ordoñez.

"Felix Zamora del Porrena, at your service. You have come to give yourself up, maybe?"

"*Mierda,*" Ordoñez said.

Zamora laughed, one short bark. He looked at Faver.

"And you, *gringo.* I knew you'd cause me problems. Why don't I have Javier kill you?"

Faver grinned back at him. He'd seen Fernando in the doorway behind the *jefe,* his broad, placid face showing no hint of coming violence. It looked like Zamora was just being playful.

"Two reasons. First, you're interested in what I have to say." He rubbed his leg near the top of his boot. "Second, I'd live just a little longer than you would."

"Eh?" Zamora frowned. "You're addled, *hombre. Muy loco.*"

"Maybe."

Faver shrugged, gestured carelessly with his right hand. His fingers brushed his boot top, hooked over the haft of the old bone-handled knife hidden there, drew it clear. A flip of his wrist sent it quivering into the dirt at Zamora's feet.

Fernando and Rabbit stared, too surprised to move. The one

called Javier swore and pulled his gun, but a gesture from Zamora froze him. The bandit chief had neither moved nor changed expression.

"Your boys ought to search a man before they start threatening him," Faver said. "Now, can we stop playing games and talk?"

Zamora stood motionless for another moment, then laughed his humorless laugh. He bent and retrieved the knife, tossed it back to Faver. Then he strode across to the table and sat down opposite Ordoñez.

"Your *gringo* friend likes to take chances, *Capitán*. But he makes sense, some of the time. Let's talk."

The night was well along by the time Faver finished explaining his plan. Nobody interrupted him, though Javier kept moving restlessly. At the end, both Ordoñez and Zamora shook their heads, but neither seemed to want to be the first to speak. Zamora finally broke the silence.

"This is foolish. You ask us to work together. Do you think I'd put my boys into the hands of"—he gestured at Ordoñez—"of the *soldados?*"

"I can't see you have much choice," Faver countered. "Captain, what happens if you don't stop the hostiles soon?"

"Well, as I told you, I must report that the Indians are beyond my control. Mexico City will send regular troops against them, and against the bandits as well."

"And ruin your precious reputation!" Javier snarled. "That's what worries you! But you'll never live to call in those lice!"

Faver laughed, watching Zamora.

"Kill us, and you'll get the regulars that much sooner, as soon as the government finds out their local commander's been killed." He looked at Javier. "Maybe the *rurales,* too, if you'd like that better."

Javier stiffened, scowled. The dreaded rural police were nothing to joke about. He fingered his pistol uneasily for a moment, then turned away.

"I still don't understand," Zamora said. "If the Apaches are as smart as you say, why should they fall into an ambush?"

"They need guns. If they hear you're getting a shipment of

rifles, it should be enough to bring them out. They'll be suspicious, but they'll look it over. And I can see that they hear about it."

"This will also bring us out," Zamora observed. "We'll be with the wagon, helpless if the soldiers decide to turn on us. Why do you want my men to help you?"

"Nantahe isn't a fool," Faver said patiently. "If it looks like a trap, he'll know it's a trap. It has to be your bunch. When Nantahe jumps you, the troopers will hit him with everything. One big punch."

Zamora stroked his moustache, his narrow face thoughtful. "One blow—*un golpe terrífico*—while they're busy with us. There will really be rifles?"

Ordoñez answered. "There will. Faver arranged it somehow." His eyes went from Zamora to Faver and back. "I don't like any of this. But if you agree, you'd need to send only a few men, five or six, with the wagon. And there will be no treachery"—his voice hardened—"on our part, at least. I give my word."

"Your word!" Javier sneered. "You don't expect the *jefe* to believe that?"

The bandit chief didn't answer right away, and Javier stared at him in disbelief.

"*Jefe,* you don't trust them?"

"I'm not sure."

"The word of the soldiers is so much filth in the street. And this *gringo—Jefe,* let me shoot them!"

"*¡Madre de Dios!*" Without warning, Zamora leaped to his feet, his fist crashing down on the table. "How am I supposed to think when all you want is to shoot people? Out! Get out of here! Fernando, get him out!"

Faver expected a violent reaction, but the bodyguard surprised him. He straightened, glaring at Zamora, then flung away from the table. Shaking off Fernando's restraining hand, he stalked out of the room, slamming the battered door behind him.

"A single blow," Zamora murmured, sinking back into his seat as if nothing had happened. "But how will the troops follow us?"

"They won't." Faver had explained it all before, but now Zamora was really listening. He's going to bite, Faver thought. He's really going to bite.

"Look." He smoothed a map out on the table. "You'll pick up

the rifles here, on the Rio Grande. You'll follow the road along here, then strike out south toward—toward the mountains. There are two good spots for an ambush on that route. Nantahe will hit you at one of them."

"If he comes at all."

Ordoñez leaned forward and pointed. "My troop will leave La Morita the day before, riding south. In the night, we'll circle back. There's a canyon, here, between Faver's two ambush sites. We'll wait there with scouts out to watch, and we'll come when we're needed."

"Or a little late, maybe?"

The captain's face went white. He rose, fists balled at his sides. "I gave my word."

"And you'll have the rifles," Faver added quickly. "He can't wait too long. He can't let the Apaches get that shipment."

"Yes, we'll have the rifles." Zamora stood up, stretched his arms wide. He yawned. *"Ai,* it's late to argue these things. Why didn't you bring some whiskey, *gringo,* if you want to talk all night?"

"Jefe, I could—" Rabbit began timidly, but Zamora waved him to silence.

"It might work. And we need to try something. I've lost enough men to the Apaches already. But my boys won't like working with the soldiers. You saw how Javier felt."

Faver shrugged. "Well, if Javier gives the orders in your outfit—"

"I didn't say that." Zamora's voice was still mild, but there was a hint of feeling, the first Faver had seen there, behind his shallow eyes. "No. We'll do it."

"Captain?" Faver asked.

Ordoñez was silent. He rubbed a hand across his face. "If my superiors ever found out about this," he murmured. He looked up. "No, never mind. I agree."

"One thing," Zamora said briskly. "I want some kind of—what is it?—insurance."

"What do you mean?" Ordoñez demanded.

This was it, Faver thought. He could see the captain getting ready to balk, the whole careful setup falling through. He started to interrupt, to try making peace somehow. Before he could speak, Zamora jerked a thumb at him.

"Faver. He planned all this. He rides with the wagon, with my boys. Whatever happens to us, something just a little worse happens to him."

The captain's tense face relaxed into a smile, his first of the evening. "An excellent idea. Then he can keep an eye on your men. Agreed, *amigo?*"

The question was directed at Faver, and this time he didn't have to wonder about Ordoñez's tone. It was coldly mocking, as if the captain were really enjoying the situation. But Zamora was right. Faver had planned the operation, and there was only one answer he could make.

"Sure. That's fine."

Still on his feet, Zamora glanced toward Fernando and Rabbit. They filed quickly outside.

"Anything more? No? Then you'll let me know when all is ready." The muddy eyes rested on Faver. "You know how to reach me. *Adiós.*" Then, as an afterthought, "Don't, *por favor,* come outside until we ride away. One of my boys on the hill might make a mistake."

He left. A few moments later, hoofbeats sounded on the packed earth of the trail. Ordoñez sighed.

"A bad bargain."

"Maybe."

"Well, there's no point in arguing it now. How soon can you be ready?"

"Not long." Faver stood up and stretched to relieve cramped muscles. It had grown cold in the little room while they talked. A fitful wind picked at the chinks in the *jacal*'s walls, sending eddies of dust swirling through the open doorway.

"It won't take long to set it up," Faver repeated. "A week or two. Are you in a hurry now?"

Ordoñez nodded soberly. "I'm in a hurry to see the last of you."

"Yeah." Faver laughed without much humor. "I noticed. The one thing you and Zamora agreed on is that I should be in the way of the first bullet that comes along."

"It's your trap," Ordoñez told him. "Zamora is risking his men. I'm risking my career and—" He pulled up sharply, hesitated, went on. "—And perhaps something that means a great deal more to me. But that remains to be settled. Maybe we felt you should risk something as well."

He rose and retrieved his pistol from the floor where Rabbit had left it.

"We can go now."

He went out, his footsteps fading toward the place they'd left the horses. For a minute longer, Faver sat staring at the planks of the table, his fingers lightly tracing the scar on his cheek.

Maybe Estella had been right, in spite of his protests. Maybe he was using them all, endangering other lives to get his revenge. But he didn't see any other way the hostiles could be stopped. At least this time the risk would fall on those best qualified to take it, on the Guardia and on Zamora's bandits.

And he would be there with them.

He blew out the single candle and followed Ordoñez out into the night.

CHAPTER 17

Braswell had set up the delivery. He'd made an advance payment, and the final price had been settled beforehand, but there were customs among the smugglers along the Rio Grande, and neither the gunrunners nor Zamora's bandits seemed willing to violate them.

On the south side of the river, Jess Faver sat motionless on his horse. He wore an old sombrero. A woolen serape was thrown about his shoulders, partly for disguise and partly for protection against the chill morning mist, and he held his rifle cradled in the crook of his arm. Javier and Rabbit flanked him to left and right. Across on the Texas side, perhaps forty yards away, four Anglos sat equally still, each group eyeing the other suspiciously.

There was a low, muddy sandbar in mid-river, halfway between the two lines of men. Fernando and the spokesman for the gunrunners squatted together there, talking softly. Occasionally, a sudden gesture or a voice raised in anger would send a ripple of motion through one of the little knots of gunmen. Then the talk would pick up again, and the guards would settle back into their watchful silence.

To Faver, the whole thing seemed unreal. It was like a play, or some Apache ceremonial he only half understood. It seemed necessary, though, and it should be awfully convincing if any of Nantahe's bunch were watching.

If. He let his attention wander, first to the tangled willow breaks on the far side of the river, then to the swirling brown water that separated him from his old life. There was no if in his mind. He could feel the tension in the changed rhythm of the land, in the first stirrings of the dawn breeze as it scattered the mist along the river. He couldn't have explained it to any white man, not even Randall, but he knew.

Nantahe was out. He would try for the rifles. One way or the other, it would end today. Faver knew. He wondered if Nantahe knew it too.

Out on the narrow sandbar, Fernando stood up. He spat in the palm of his right hand and held it out to the other man. The gunrunner rose and shook his hand, palms coming together with an audible smack. Some of the stiffness left the watchers. Horses moved restlessly, pawing at the sand as reins were slackened. Fernando turned and waved.

"Javier! The gold!"

Javier slid his rifle back into its boot and clucked to his horse. He splashed through the shallow water out to the bar, leaned down to hand a canvas bag to Fernando.

The smuggler waved in his turn. A wagon drawn by two horses waddled from the screen of willows down to the river's edge. Two of the gunrunners rode over to help guide the horses across. The wagon lurched across the rocky bottom of the ford. At midstream, the driver pulled up the horses and waited while Javier swung into the back. Two or three minutes passed while the bandit ducked under the canvas cover and examined the load. Then he emerged onto the seat beside the driver.

"*Bueno*. Two cases, with ammunition."

Fernando handed over the bag. The gunrunner looked inside, poured part of the contents into his palm. He nodded. The wagon driver swung up behind one of the riders and went back to the far side, while Javier took the lines and drove the wagon across. Fernando came back, leading Javier's horse, and both groups faded cautiously into the thickets along the river.

"Fifty pesos less than we'd agreed on," Fernando boasted. "Maybe our trader friend will get some of his money back."

Faver reined up beside him. "He'll never miss fifty pesos. Keep it to buy Teresa a new dress when we get back."

Fernando didn't answer right away. The big man had been strangely moody ever since Faver had joined up with the band the night before. Now he looked away, down the dusty trail to the south.

"You better ride in the wagon, *gringo*. It's best if your Indian doesn't recognize you, if he's around. Rabbit, you ride ahead, and Javier can drive. Let's move."

The bandits set a brisk pace—as brisk, at least, as the wagon could manage in the rough country below the river. Faver rode on the wagon box, his rifle within reach under the canvas cover, his horse and Javier's tied to the tailboard. A mile from the ford, three more bandits rode out to join them. They spread out on the flanks, far enough apart to make poor targets.

Just right, Faver thought as the party moved deeper into the hills. The escort was strong enough to look convincing, but nothing that the Apaches wouldn't figure they could handle. Braswell and Zamora had done their jobs well. The soldiers under Ordoñez should be in position in the box canyon by now, waiting for word that the trap had sprung. Things could still go wrong, but they'd done all the planning they could. The rest depended on Nantahe.

For a moment, Faver worried that Nantahe might sense the trap, might feel the same undercurrent of danger that Faver felt in the desert breeze. Then he shook his head, dismissed the idea. It was strange, he thought. Nantahe, Zamora, Braswell, even Ordoñez—everybody who might have reason to want him dead—all tied in at the finish.

The miles unrolled under the wagon's iron tires. The sun shouldered its way above the eastern ridges, burned away the morning chill. A brisk, gusty wind whipped at the brush along the trail. Javier drove in stony silence, broken only by mutterings about the dust of the thrice-damned road, and Faver was content to let him be. He scanned the ridges and skylines, looking for any hint that they were being followed, any sign of the Apaches. He saw nothing, but his certainty was unshaken: Nantahe was out there.

"*Ai, gringo.*" Fernando pulled up alongside the wagon. "Maybe another hour to the first place you thought *los indios* might jump us. You think the troopers are where they're supposed to be?"

"*¿Quién sabe?* But why not?"

"Well, they might decide to trap us after all." The bandit rubbed his bristly chin. "I think maybe Capitán Ordoñez doesn't love you."

Javier chuckled, but Faver didn't see anything funny about it. If Fernando wasn't careful, he'd spook the whole bunch with his worries. Faver let his annoyance show in his voice.

"The captain will be there, with every man he has. One blow, just like your boss said. If your boys don't run out when the shooting starts, everything will be fine."

Fernando gazed at him a moment longer, a troubled frown on his face. Then he spurred ahead abruptly and left the wagon behind. Insulted, Faver supposed, and worried. That wasn't like Fernando, but maybe he had reason today. He was certainly right about one thing: the captain didn't seem to love Faver. His farewell before Faver left La Morita had been as cold as Estella's had been warm.

The girl had come down to the plaza just at sundown. Faver was leading out his horse, ready to ride out. She stopped in front of him, a step away, looking up into his face.

"I knew something was happening. You've been gone so much, and Luis—" She shrugged, went on. "You're going after him, aren't you?"

Faver didn't have to guess who she meant. "I've always been after him."

"But this is different. I know it. I—I am sorry for what I said that night. I was wrong. Please don't do something foolish because of it."

"It's not that," Faver assured her gently. "And maybe you weren't so far wrong. When I come back, we'll have to talk about some things."

She stood on tiptoe, one hand on his arm, and quickly pressed her lips to his.

"When you come back, I'll be ready."

Only after she'd gone and he turned toward the barracks did he see Ordoñez standing in the shadows outside his quarters. He didn't know how much the captain had heard, and Ordoñez didn't give any indication.

"The troop is ready," he said. "We move tomorrow, and we'll be in position late tomorrow night. See that your bandits do their part."

"They will. Trust me."

"No." Ordoñez apparently didn't see the hand Faver offered. "Understand me. You're doing this for your own reasons, and I think you'd sacrifice my men or"—he glanced quickly in the direction Estella had gone—"or anyone else for those reasons. I trust you no more than I trust Zamora."

Slowly, Faver withdrew his hand. "Maybe you're right," he said quietly. He should have been angry, he knew, but for some reason he wasn't. He mounted, then reined the horse back, unwilling to leave it like this with Ordoñez.

"Captain, I—" There was no way to say what he wanted to. "Good luck."

The captain didn't answer, and Faver touched his spurs to the buckskin's flanks, moving out on the road south.

Up ahead, Fernando raised his hand. Faver shook off his memories impatiently, came back to alertness. If he expected to see either the captain or Estella again, he'd better keep his mind on his work.

Javier hauled back on the lines and the wagon jolted to a stop. Leaning forward, elbows on his knees, he looked ahead.

"Up there," he said. "It's not far now."

The wagon had topped a low hogback. Ahead, the trail went down in a series of switchbacks to the floor of a narrow valley, then turned south and curved out of sight. Faver recognized the place from the captain's map. A little way beyond the curve, the road would plunge into a narrow, sheer-walled canyon. It was a good spot for an ambush.

The bandit loosened his pistol in its holster, gave Faver a wolfish grin. "*Bueno, gringo*. It won't be long."

"I hope not."

Fernando raised his arm in the signal to move. Javier kicked the brake to check it, then snapped the lines across the horses' backs. The heavy wagon began to jolt down the trail.

Suddenly, Faver was uneasy. He fought off the urge to reach back for his rifle; the canyon was still miles away. Instead, he braced himself against the footboard and tried to decide what had changed. Some little thing, maybe, something said or done. He couldn't place it, but his certainty of a fated meeting with Nantahe was gone. Something was wrong.

He frowned. There was one thing. On his way to the bandit camp, he'd turned aside to run an errand, an errand no one else knew about. It was something he'd had to do. He wondered now if he'd done it only to prove Estella and the captain wrong about him.

He'd ridden back along the familiar trail into the hills to the canyon where Juana's wickiup stood. For once, her medicine seemed to have failed her, for she wasn't expecting him. She was just rising from the creek bank when he rode in, a heavy water jar balanced on her shoulder. She saw him and started, almost dropping the jar. Lowering it painfully to the ground, she hobbled to meet him.

"You did come back." Her eyes showed wonder. "I thought—" She broke off and stared at him closely, then gave her cackling laugh. "You're not quite so pretty now. They thought you'd died."

"I'll bet."

"Get down. Let your horse graze." She gestured toward the wickiup. "I have too much stew cooking for just an old woman. And where's my cow?"

Faver didn't dismount. He leaned on the saddle horn and looked down at her. "I didn't bring it, Grandmother. But I brought some good advice."

"Just like a white-eye! Promise cows and give advice."

"The *piñon* nuts are ready to be gathered, Grandmother. You should have some for the winter."

Slowly, the old woman came closer. She reached up and touched the buckskin's withers with a gnarled hand. Her eyes searched his face.

"It's winter now, white-eye. It's too late for *piñon* nuts. They fell months ago."

"They're ready to be gathered," Faver repeated. "I saw some good ones in the mountains to the south. Maybe your grandson would take you to look for them."

Juana's expression didn't change, but she nodded slowly. "That would take him away from those cut-offs for a while, at least," she murmured. "I'll ask him."

"Ask him soon. Today." The woman stepped back, and he reined his horse around. "Good-bye, Grandmother. Thanks for your help."

He rode back the way he'd come in. The last time he looked, just before the trail took him out of sight, she was still standing motionless, looking after him.

The wagon jolted to a stop and Faver looked up sharply. Fernando and the others were clustered beside the trail. A pair of deep-cut ruts, probably leading to some isolated *jacal,* split off to the west down a rocky draw. Javier reined in the team and looped the lines over the brake lever. Faver leaned past him to look at Fernando.

"*¿Amigo, qué pasa?*"

The big man gazed at him sadly, shook his head. "What's the—?" Faver began, but then he knew. He froze into immobility at the sound of a pistol being cocked almost at his elbow.

Rabbit was beside the wagon box, the muzzle of his gun only inches from Faver's belly. Javier reached across to wrench Faver's pistol from its holster.

"I'm sorry, *gringo*," Fernando said. "It can't be helped. This is business."

Javier produced a length of rope, bound Faver's hands, then picked up the reins again. With a sigh, Fernando led out. The column turned away from the main trail and off into the hills.

There really was a *jacal* a mile or so in, but it was long abandoned, its roof fallen in and the adobe walls slowly melting back into the earth. Zamora was waiting nearby, with fresh horses and a few of his men. He frowned when he saw Faver.

"Fernando, I told you— No, never mind." He stood looking at Faver. "Thanks for the guns, *gringo*." He smiled, but his eyes were as dead as ever. "Too bad you know so much about my friends and my little village, no? We will return by another way, and not annoy the soldiers. Zamora couldn't take the chance."

"You're taking one now," Faver told him softly.

"Shut up, *gringo*." Javier cuffed him across the face. "Keep quiet, and maybe you live a little longer."

The bandits harnessed a fresh team to the wagon and pressed on up the side trail, a man Faver didn't know taking Javier's seat on the wagon box. Jammed into a corner of the high spring seat, the cords cutting into his wrists, Faver watched bleakly. The bandits apparently never learned; his hunting knife made a comforting bulge in the top of his boot. It was only a matter of time before he found the chance to use it.

This might be his day to die, but he wouldn't die at the hands of these fish-eaters. He'd get free soon enough, and he'd live to pull out Zamora's guts six inches at a time for spoiling his trap.

Fernando and Javier were riding point, and the other bandits made a semblance of covering flanks and rear. They were pleased with their clever trick on the soldiers, and they obviously weren't looking for trouble. At a halt to rest the horses, someone broke out a bottle of whiskey. When they moved on again, the guards were noisier and even less watchful.

Waiting for the moment to make his break, Faver had almost forgotten everything else. When the wagon topped a long rise and halted for a moment, he scanned the land ahead, watching for a chance to slip away before Zamora decided to finish him.

Before long he found the place. His trained eye took in the rocky creek bed, the broad gravel bar with a green rivulet seeping along against the far bank. The wagon road slanted down the ridge, crossed the creek, and vanished into stands of salt cedar and river cane. There were flats on the far side, thickly studded with low, heavy underbrush. That should do, he thought. You could hide an army down there.

The realization hit him like a cold fist in the belly. His anger at Zamora vanished, replaced by a moment of sheer panic, then by an uncontrollable urge to laugh. He grinned, and the driver looked at him in surprise.

Zamora hadn't spoiled the plan. The Apaches would have had scouts out to see the wagon leave the road—and Nantahe and Chicuelo were adaptable.

No, the bandits hadn't ruined things. Faver would get his ambush. The only ones missing would be Ordoñez and the troops.

CHAPTER 18

Faver didn't take time to plan. If he was right, they were out of time. Already, Javier and Fernando had splashed across the creek and were mounting the cutbank to the flats beyond. Zamora was halfway down the ridge, with most of the other bandits clustered around him. Then the driver snapped the lines and the wagon began to move.

The crated rifles had been loaded over the wagon's rear axle, and the part of the bed just below the seat was empty. As the wagon made its lurching descent, Faver slipped off the seat. Hoping it looked accidental, he fell heavily into the bed.

"Look out, *hombre,*" the driver snapped. He was riding the brake with his left foot, and both hands were busy with the lines. He tried to get one hand free to reach for his gun, but the horses wouldn't let him. He settled for glaring at Faver.

"Don't try anything. I'll kill you now."

Faver moaned. "My arm! I think it's broken."

His doubled legs had taken part of the shock, but his bad shoulder had slammed hard into the footboard. That didn't matter, though. The knife was out of his boot, hidden from the driver by his body, already working on the cords on his wrists.

"How could I try anything? How does your boss expect me to hold on with my hands tied this way?"

"Maybe he doesn't much care. Be still."

His hands were free. He flexed his fingers, tightened his grip on the knife. If he had to, he could reach the driver with one lunge, even with his feet bound.

The wagon swayed, came out on level ground. The bandit slacked off on the reins. Grinning, he nudged Faver with the toe of his boot.

"You just lie there, *gringo*. It's easy to watch you. We'll fix your arm up fine, before—"

He never finished. The wagon's tires had crunched into the gravel of the creek bed and, as if that was a signal, a single shot crashed out in the stillness.

Faver had a fraction of a second to see the driver's grin freeze into an agonized grimace, to see his body jerk under the impact of the bullet. Then the man tumbled forward under the wheels, his scream drowned by a clatter of shots that seemed to come from all directions.

Freeing his feet with a sweep of the knife, Faver dived for the reins. The horses had spooked, and he gave them their head. He was in the open here, totally exposed. He had to reach cover.

Ahead, he saw the two point men. Javier had pulled up short when the first shot came. A moment later an Apache warrior, his oiled body plastered with trail dust, sprang from the ground almost at the bandit's stirrup. Javier tried to curb his rearing mount with one hand while he clawed for his pistol with the other. He'd barely cleared leather when an upthrusting lance tore through his right arm and into his chest.

Fernando, quicker and luckier, rode down the first man who came at him. Then he clapped spurs to his mount and wheeled, driving desperately back toward the creek. Bullets kicked up dirt around him as other Apaches broke cover to open fire.

Faver hauled back on the reins, trying to regain control. There was no escape that way, probably none in any direction. His only chance lay with the bandits, or what was left of them.

Caught in the open by the first fire, half of them had been shot down before they could react. Zamora had the survivors down behind the cutbank of the creek, knee-deep in the water, firing to cover Fernando's retreat. The bandit chief looked back, waved his arm at Faver.

"*Gringo,* here! Bring the wagon!"

Faver saw what he meant. It was a bad position, open to fire from the rear and from the willow thickets downstream. The wagon would offer some protection, if he could put it in the right place.

He hauled the team into a turn. A bandit, still mounted, came from nowhere and spurred parallel to the near horse, trying to help. He was hit and fell away. Then the off-side horse of the team screamed and threw itself sideways in the traces, blood pumping down its flank.

The wagon swayed, started to go over. Faver made a desperate grab for his rifle. He had a momentary glimpse of Fernando scrambling to safety, of Zamora's startled face as the wagon bore down on him. Then he jumped.

He hit the ground running, stumbled to his knees, and lunged forward again as the wagon crashed over behind him. Someone grabbed him under the arms and yanked him along, and then he was panting against the damp sand of the bank.

"Welcome, *gringo!*" Zamora called. "I was afraid you wouldn't make it." He knelt behind the bank, looking across at Faver. "You were right, I shouldn't have tried my—what do you say?— double-cross. No hard feelings, eh?"

Faver stared at him. The little bandit's eyes were bright, alive with an almost joyful excitement.

"Look out!" somebody yelled before Faver could answer. "Here they come!"

At least a dozen warriors were charging down on the little pocket. Faver was surprised to find he still held the rifle. He levered a shell into it and fired, hearing the boom of Zamora's big pistol in the background. The bandit beside him spun around suddenly and pitched into the water, but the Apaches were meeting more resistance than they'd expected. One threw up his arms and rolled in the dust. Another warrior caught him around the waist and dragged him to cover, and then the Indians were gone.

Fernando rose to his knees and peered around, unbelieving. Even to Faver's eyes, there was no sign of the Apaches. The wagon was on its side behind them, one of the horses still kicking feebly in a tangle of harness. Zamora dashed across and fired two quick shots. The movement stopped. The bandit leader ducked back into the shelter of the bank.

"Fernando, how many of us left?"

Fernando slipped his hands beneath the shoulders of the man who'd been hit beside Faver. He lifted him from the water, peered into his face for a moment, then let him fall back. He shrugged.

"As you see, *Jefe*. Sermio and Rabbit are at the back of the wagon, and somebody was shooting from over by those rocks. The rest—" He shrugged again.

"*Bueno*." Zamora raised his voice. "Juan! Artemio! Where are you, *muchachos?*"

Someone answered from the brush off to the right. Zamora nodded. "Seven, maybe eight of us." He lifted his head over the cutbank, yanked up his pistol and snapped three shots into the brush.

"Anything there?"

The bandit chief stared into the thicket for a moment, then slid back down the bank. He began to reload his pistol.

"I don't think so. I thought something moved. What are they waiting for?"

"That rush scattered them some," Faver said. "Nantahe and Chicuelo will need a little time to get them organized again. And they want to let us think about it for a while."

Zamora laughed. He sounded as if he meant it. "I'm thinking about it. Fernando, keep watch."

He crawled across to the wagon, used his knife to slash away the tatters of the canvas top. One of the ammunition boxes had broken open. Zamora scooped up a handful of brass-jacketed .44 cartridges.

"We've got bullets, anyway. Take some, *gringo*."

Faver filled his shirt pockets, passed more to Fernando and the other two bandits. All three had held on to their rifles, and Braswell had evidently managed to keep everything the same caliber.

"We can probably hold them for a while," Zamora went on. "*Gringo,* what—?"

There was a puff of smoke high on the ridge behind them, just to the left of the trail they'd come down. A bullet thunked solidly into the bed of the wagon. A second rifle began firing from lower down, then a third. Fernando ducked lower as bullets pocked the top of the cutbank.

"*¡Madre de Dios!* They're everywhere!"

Faver angled his rifle past the dead horses, put a bullet in the general area of the third marksman. Because of the wagon, the Apaches couldn't quite get a clear shot at any of the defenders, but their fire would be deadly to anyone who moved far to either side.

The first rifle spoke again, its sound somehow louder and flatter than the others. "That's a Springfield," Faver muttered. "Nantahe."

"What? Oh, your pet Apache. He's up there?"

"With my carbine, probably. He'll be running the fight from there. He's got three or four braves with him, and most of the others out in front of us."

The firing slackened for a moment, picked up again. Zamora swore. He moved quickly back to the bank.

"I think they're going to try another rush. Rabbit, move over and watch that island downstream. They have somebody in the willows there."

"*Bueno, Jefe.*"

"*Gringo,* if you could shoot a little at those on the ridge, it would be welcome. I don't want to tell you what to do, see?"

Faver grinned and kicked a shell into the rifle. "In that case, *amigo,* I'll be glad to."

The third rifleman was near a little juniper tree. It made a convenient marker, and Faver could work on him without exposing himself to the others. He set the sights on the base of the tree, adjusted for uphill shooting, and began search fire.

One shot at the tree. One five yards to the left, then five yards to the right. One above and one below and back to the tree. Reload and start over. The Marlin didn't have the solid feel of his lost Springfield, but it was accurate enough—and there was plenty of ammunition.

The fire from the juniper slackened almost as soon as his bullets started plowing up the hillside. After the first few rounds, it stopped altogether. Faver couldn't see his man, but he must be coming close—maybe too close for one of Nantahe's undisciplined *broncos.*

He'd just shifted to the left for the fourth time when he saw movement near the tree. It might have been a man, turning, trying to reach deeper cover. Faver shifted his aim and emptied the magazine at the spot, gouts of dirt rising where the bullets hit. The last shots went into a big beavertail cactus and ripped it apart, sending one of the platelike leaves flying far off to one side. For a moment longer, the cactus shook and trembled. Then everything was still.

Faver had heard the shots behind him, the cries of the Apaches, one short gasp of pain nearby, but he hadn't looked back. He had his own part of the fight to worry about.

Now the firing had stopped, and there was silence except for Zamora's soft cursing. The little bandit sat against the cutbank, leaning back heavily against the pocked sand. His pistol lay in a niche scooped out just above the level of the creek, and both hands were clamped around his thigh so tightly that the knuckles showed white. Below his clenched fingers, blood feathered out into the flowing green water.

"One of the sons of a whore can shoot." He laid his head back against the bank. "I think they got our two boys out in the brush, too."

Fernando sidled across to him. "*Sí, Jefe.* I saw Juan try to run from there." He knelt and pried one of Zamora's hands loose. "This is bad. I'll make a tourniquet for the bleeding."

"It's nothing." Zamora grimaced and reached for the pistol with his free hand. "But we don't play games with *gringos* anymore, *chico*. Never."

One of the riflemen opened up again, and Faver rolled over to look for him.

"Ordoñez must've heard the shooting," he said over his shoulder. "He's probably on his way here right now. If we can stay alive long enough, he'll bail us out."

Zamora laughed harshly. "Listen, *gringo,* Ordoñez has you and me here, and your little *dulce* is back at home waiting for him. Maybe he don't want to find us— ¿*Cómo?*"

"He'll be here. I know him."

"You knew that Apache, too. And if I had that Estella—"

"I said he'll be here. Watch those bushes on the right."

He twisted around and fired at the distant sniper, but his mind was busy with Zamora's words. He'd been confident the captain would keep his part of the bargain. Deception was no part of his nature, and Estella would probably see through any attempt. The bandits had changed all that, though. The trap had been sprung in the wrong place, far from the waiting troops. If Ordoñez wanted an excuse for being late, he had it.

All Faver could count on was the captain's sense of honor—and a man's sense of honor, he knew, could be pretty flexible.

The Apaches tried a rush an hour later. Faver moved to the cutbank to help Fernando and Zamora, while Rabbit and the other bandit kept up a steady fire at the ridge and the willow island. The attack was halfhearted and fell apart without coming too close. Faver thought he saw Chicuelo urging on the others, but the scout vanished before he could get a shot at him.

"Don't they know we're only five?" Zamora muttered. "Why don't they come on?"

"They don't want to lose any more men," Faver said. "Bad for morale. And they're willing to wait. They don't know there's any reason to hurry."

"There isn't." Zamora closed his eyes. His thin face was pinched. "I should have left you for the buzzards, *gringo*." He thought a moment, laughed. "But what a fight we'd have missed, eh, Fernando?"

"I wouldn't mind very much, *Jefe*."

"Maybe— Look out! They're moving around out there."

"They won't come again this soon," Faver said. "They'll let the long-range fire work on us while the rest are slipping as close as they can get. When they're ready, they'll all hit us at once."

"*Madre de Dios*. Well, if that one shows himself again, I'll hit him first."

They waited, firing occasionally at the riflemen or at some sound, real or imagined, from the thickets in front of them. It had been past noon when the fight began. Now the sun was settling lower. The shadows of sage and creosote bushes lengthened, began to merge together.

"Another hour and we can't see them," Zamora said.

"They won't wait another hour. Get set."

The volume of fire from the ridge had suddenly increased, and now shots were coming from the far bank as well, off to the left of the island. Sermio and Rabbit cringed back into the shelter of the wagon, unable to answer the fusillade. Whatever happened, they were effectively pinned down.

"Over there!" Zamora yelled, but the warning wasn't needed. Apaches were running through the brush, dropping flat to fire, leaping up to move again.

Faver shoved the rifle barrel up over the cutbank and was met by a storm of bullets that made him duck back. Someone was shooting from out on the flats, a cool and accurate fire at anything that moved along the bank. Fernando popped up and fired twice, then was driven back to cover. Then the shooting slackened, the Apaches holding back to avoid hitting their own men.

"Now! Get them!"

Faver shot at a big warrior who'd appeared almost at the lip of the cutbank, saw him fall backward. Zamora was struggling to gain his feet, his hurt leg giving under him. An Apache lunged at him. Fernando shot the Indian down, then turned to grapple with a warrior who'd dropped into the creek beside him.

Downstream, the sporadic gunfire built into a continuous, rolling crackle. Faver wondered what had happened, but he didn't have time to look. The rifle's hammer clicked on empty, and he swung the barrel at an Apache coming at him with a knife.

The warrior ducked under the blow and drove in. His shoulder slammed into Faver's ribs, sending him staggering back against the bank. Rabbit leaped to help, but caught a bullet as soon as he straightened from the wagon. Half stunned, Faver made a desperate grab for the downswinging knife hand. The Apache grunted and began to force him back. Then something hit the Indian from behind and flung him aside like an empty sack.

Fernando was on his feet. The giant bandit had somehow wrenched a timber from the wrecked wagon, and was swinging it like a flail. The attackers pressed in on him so closely that their marksmen couldn't get a clear shot, and he beat them back. Zamora, sheltered behind him, frantically reloaded his pistol.

Three of their number dead at the bandit's feet, the Apaches reeled away, but more warriors were rushing to the attack, Chicuelo running with them. The roar from the willow island grew louder, and a fresh surge of Apaches burst from there.

"*Dios mío,* no!"

The cry came from Sermio, the bandit who'd held the wagon with Rabbit. He stared wildly at the oncoming warriors, then threw down his rifle and ran, dashing out into the gravel of the creek bed. He got perhaps fifteen yards, then crumpled, the flat crack of the Springfield echoing along the ridge as he fell.

"*Cabrón,*" Zamora growled. He crawled painfully to the discarded rifle, threw it to Fernando. "They got us this time, *muchachos.* No chance."

Faver recovered his rifle and swung around to meet the charge from downstream. He fired once, then again, but the Apaches were swerving aside, turning up the ridge or scattering onto the flats. It didn't make sense at first. Then he saw horsemen breaking through the willow screen, spreading out to sweep both banks of the creek. Ordoñez rode in their midst, swinging a gleaming saber over his head.

"*¡Gringo!*" Zamora's eyes were round with surprise. "They did come! The *soldados!*" He hobbled to the bank, waved his pistol. "Hey! Now come and fight! Cowards! Come and get us."

Caught between fire from the wagon and the incoming horsemen, the Apaches froze momentarily. Then they broke and ran. Faver came to his feet, tracking the fugitives with his rifle, firing smoothly. As he paused to reload, he saw Chicuelo.

The scout stood in the open, a Springfield carbine held easily in his hands. He faced the troopers, ignoring his fleeing men. He knew it was finished, Faver realized, and he wasn't going to run.

Chicuelo raised the carbine and fired. A soldier spilled from the saddle, and Chicuelo calmly flipped open the breech and shoved in another shell. He didn't have time for a second shot. A trooper on a black horse was already upon him, and Ordoñez was barely twenty yards behind.

The Apache braced himself, gripping the barrel of the carbine. As the first man closed on him, he stepped in and swung. The horse reared and Chicuelo thrust upward with the butt, clubbing the rider from the saddle. He dropped the carbine, grabbed for the dragging reins, and got one foot in a stirrup as the horse went to its knees.

Then Ordoñez was there, saber swinging in a whistling arc. It cleaved into Chicuelo's side with a shock that tore the blade from the captain's grasp. He recovered and went on past, but Faver was still watching Chicuelo.

The force of the blow had thrown him to the ground. He stirred, tried to rise, then threw himself forward, hands scrabbling for the carbine. His fingers closed on the stock, clenched, relaxed. Chicuelo lay still, his blood soaking into the thirsty earth.

The battle was over. The Apaches were on the run, troopers sweeping them to ruin on the open ground along the creek. Faver snapped from his trance, turning suddenly to look up the ridge.

Nantahe had been up there—Nantahe and a few others—and the charge had swept past them.

From the corner of his eye, he saw Fernando scoop up Zamora as if the smaller man were a doll. The big bandit loped away downstream, but Faver didn't wait to see more. He was up and running, the rifle cradled in his arms, across the gravel bar and up the slope toward Nantahe.

CHAPTER 19

He was halfway up the wagon trail when he heard the shots. At first he thought they were part of the main battle, echoing crazily among the rocks. Then he heard the roar of Nantahe's carbine and knew there was fighting somewhere ahead. He cocked the rifle and paused a moment to breathe. When he moved again, he went more slowly, watching the skyline ahead.

An Apache lay face-down beside a clump of cactus, just short of the crest. Faver approachd cautiously, finally knelt and rolled the body over. Scar's face looked up at him, the features locked into a final snarl of rage and pain. Faver straightened and moved quickly over the top of the ridge. A second warrior was dead there, outflung hand almost touching the brown-clad body of a Guardia trooper. A few yards down the slope, another soldier knelt on the ground, pale face turned toward Faver.

"*Señor—por Dios*—help me."

Faver bent over him. The trooper's uniform blouse was stained with blood, and his hands were clenched tightly against his left side. Faver eased him into a more comfortable position, then gently moved to explore the wound. A bullet had caught the man glancingly, tearing muscles, probably breaking a rib or two. It was bad enough, but surely not fatal. Faver pulled off his shirt and began tearing it into strips.

"What happened? How did you get here?"

"Capitán Ordoñez sent us ahead. We were to block any Indians who came this way." The trooper closed his eyes, breathed deeply. After a few seconds, he went on in a stronger voice. "Three came over the hill. We shot at them and they fell, but one of them had a pistol, too. When we moved—" He broke off, caught Faver's arm. "Jorge, my *compadre*. He's hurt worse than me."

Faver shook his head. "No," he said. "But you stopped two of the Apaches. Where did the third one go?"

"Up there."

Off to the west, the ridge sloped upward, first to a higher crest, then to a peak flanked by sheer rock walls. Painfully, the soldier gestured that way.

"He went up there. I think we hit him, too. He dropped something when we fired, just by those rocks."

Faver folded a part of the shirt into a pad, tied it in place with the other strips. Then he rose and crossed to the boulders. There was blood on the ground there, and scuffed marks where someone had fallen and scrambled up again. A few yards beyond, the Springfield carbine lay half-hidden in the brush.

He picked it up, running his fingers over the bullet-shattered stock.

"You hit him, all right," he murmured. Then, briskly, "Are you all right here? You have water?"

"I—yes, my canteen."

"Lie still. The captain will find you before long. Tell him I went after the Indian."

The soldier shook his head. "Don't. You better wait," he said. "He's a bad one, that *indio*."

Faver had already turned away, following the blood-spoor up the rocks. A pursued Apache would head for high ground, he thought. It had been a long hunt, and now it was almost over.

Keeping the rifle ready, he climbed steadily toward the heights until a tumbled mass of boulders blocked his way. The trail was fresh here, red spatters of blood clotting on the ground. They led off to the left, then upward again through a narrow draw that opened back among the rocks. Faver paused and listened. There was only silence ahead.

He glanced back the way he'd come. The shoulder of the mountain hid the place where he'd left the wounded trooper, but he could see the sparkle of the creek far below. The sounds of the fight had died away. He and Nantahe would be alone at the end.

The rocks ahead were made for a trap. In order to see into the draw, he would have to cross ten feet of open ground at its mouth. Nantahe might be dead in there, or he might be still climbing painfully toward the top—but he could be waiting in cover, feeling his life drain away and hoping to take one more trooper with him.

Faver gathered himself, pulse thumping with the mixture of excitement and fear that went with the stalk and the kill. Gripping the rifle tightly against his body, he took two long strides and launched himself into the open.

He hit the ground rolling, scrambling for the shelter of a boulder. No shots ripped through the silence, no bullets plowed the dust around him. Almost disappointed, he brought up the rifle to cover the rocks ahead. Then he saw Nantahe.

The Apache sat stiffly upright against the bank of the draw, a few short yards from the crest of the slope. His legs were stretched in front of him and his arms lay limp at his sides, but his right hand was locked around the butt of Faver's Remington pistol. He watched Faver with a steady, unwavering gaze.

Faver rose and moved slowly in on him. Ten feet away, he stopped and Nantahe spoke.

"A good scout, *sikisn.*" The voice was a hoarse whisper, barely audible over the wind. "I didn't expect you."

"Don't move. I'll kill you."

Nantahe's lips skinned back in what might have been meant as a smile. "If I could move, I'd have shot you."

Faver had seen the blood that soaked Nantahe's shirt. Now he looked for the first time at the damage the trooper's bullets had done. Involuntarily, his eyes widened in shock.

"Nantahe—"

A heavy slug had torn through the scout's body below the ribs. A second bullet had broken his left arm, so that a jagged edge of bone grinned whitely through the ripped fabric of his shirt. Nantahe's face was bathed in sweat, but his eyes still burned with the savage driving force that had carried him up out of the valley.

"The others?" A shudder racked him, but his expression didn't change. "Chicuelo?"

"All gone. There's only you and me."

Faver came forward, keeping the rifle leveled. For a moment, he'd almost forgotten. Now he felt again the bite of a rope across his chest, and the thirst for vengeance rose up in him.

"I'm going to take that gun. Then I'll try to patch you up a little."

"It doesn't matter."

"Yes, it does. You're tough, maybe tough enough to make it. I want you to live. I'm taking you back."

Nantahe closed his eyes. When he opened them again, they held the trapped look Faver had seen when Nantahe was in the guardhouse at Camp Bowie. The muscles of the scout's right arm tensed. The muzzle of the Remington came up an inch, then another.

Faver didn't move. The gun barrel wavered, dropped. Nantahe's shoulders slumped with exhaustion. He breathed raggedly for a moment, then raised his eyes to Faver's.

"Don't do it, brother. Let me die here."

Grimly, Faver shook his head. He knew what the words had cost Nantahe, but he took no pleasure in the knowledge.

"I turned you loose," he said. "I started this, and I'm going to finish it." He reached out, knocked the pistol away. "Don't call me brother. You said I was just another white-eye."

Nantahe's face changed. His jaw tightened and his eyes burned with the implacable hatred of the renegade. "Then do what another white-eye would," he whispered, and there was a note of pleading in his voice. "Kill me!"

Faver caught his breath suddenly, then let it out. Reflected in Nantahe's face, he saw his own hatred—the bitter, corrosive hatred between white and Apache that stretched back and back, into years before either of them had been born. That was what had destroyed Nantahe and could easily destroy him as well.

He was responsible for releasing Nantahe, but he wasn't responsible for the hatred—only for what he let it do to him. Now he had a choice to make, a choice that went beyond Nantahe. He could follow neither the white nor the Apache road. He had to make his own way, and this first step had to be one he could live with all his days.

Slowly, he came to his feet. He stepped backward, swinging up the rifle.

"Good-bye, brother," he said softly, seeing Nantahe's answering smile as his finger closed on the trigger.

Along the hogback of the mountain, a drooping juniper clung precariously to a patch of soil between two flat slabs of rock.

Faver buried Nantahe beneath the twisted branches. There was no deerskin to wrap the body, no treasured belongings to put in the grave. Faver laid the old pistol beneath Nantahe's folded hands— not because the Apache's spirit would need it, but as an offering, a sign of grief at the loss of a brother and a way of life. Then he carried rocks until his hands were torn and bloody and his chest was streaked with sweat-gummed dirt and nothing showed under the juniper except a long, low mound.

The sun was well behind the mountains when he finished. He stood for a moment, arms hanging loosely by his sides. The ridge sloped away to the north, toward the Rio Grande. Touched with the orange light of sunset, the Chisos Mountains rose, ghostlike, thirty miles away. Between Faver and the mountains, running west to east until the black mouth of Mariscal Canyon swallowed it, the river made a silver thread across the desert.

"Sleep well, *sikisn*," Faver murmured. Already, the Apache words seemed foreign on his tongue. "All debts are paid."

A sudden gust of wind stirred the branches of the juniper, dried the rivulets of sweat on Faver's skin. Riding high and free, the wind swept toward the distant river, sending ripples of pale gold through the dry grass of the hillsides. Faver shivered, only partly from the chill, as he turned toward the darkness of the valley floor.

He came down the mountain loosely, moving without haste or caution. There was no urgency now, and he was tired. Beneath the weariness, he felt neither joy nor sorrow, only a quiet content-ment, as though he'd been a long time in prison and now was free. One of the captain's patrols must have found the bodies and the wounded trooper, because points of light showed on the slopes below him. Faintly on the rising wind, he heard voices calling his name. After a while, he answered.

Faver awoke at first light. He was in an unfamiliar bedroll on a nest of soft leaves, and the bleached canvas of a shelter tent stretched over him. Vaguely, he remembered meeting with a Guar-dia search party the night before, remembered his mixture of pleasure and relief at seeing Ordoñez' thin, intense face. There had been some talk, but that was all hazy. He must have been more tired than he'd thought.

He rolled over and sat up, running his fingers through his tangled hair. He'd gotten a shirt from someplace, a plain white peasant's smock, but he didn't remember that, either.

"So, you're finally awake. Coffee?"

Ordoñez sat on a rock beside the tent flap, freshly shaven, his uniform as neat as if he'd been on parade. Faver rubbed his own stubbly chin and grinned.

"Please."

He wriggled out of the tent and stood up, feeling the separate aches and pains as he stretched. He accepted a steaming cup of coffee from a trooper and sipped it.

"We can't offer you much of a breakfast," Ordoñez said. "We'll be moving soon. As you can see, I've already sent most of the troop back to La Morita."

Faver looked toward the camp. Half a dozen *soldados* moved about purposefully, rolling blankets or tending cooking fires under the eye of Sergeant Fuentes. Two more men stood guard over the picketed horses. They held their rifles ready, Faver noted, and their eyes flicked restlessly among the rocks of the canyon walls. Today, they were soldiers—not as good as they thought they were, but plenty good enough.

"And you stayed behind to find me?" Faver asked. "I didn't know you were that interested."

Ordoñez smiled. "It wasn't entirely altruistic. You went after Nantahe. Did you get him?"

Faver hesitated, then realized what was holding him back. Apache custom forbade mention of a dead warrior's name, forbade it with the force of law—but he was no longer bound by that law.

"Nantahe's dead. He was hit by your men late in the fight. He died on the ridge."

"I see." Ordoñez was silent for a moment. "We broke the Apaches," he said at last. "The *tropa* lost five dead and as many wounded, but we broke them. A few got away, but not enough to cause trouble." A puzzled frown crossed his face. "We found the bodies of most of the bandits, but not Zamora. He's missing."

"You could've gotten rid of all your troubles at once, *amigo,* just by waiting a little longer. That's what Zamora thought you'd do."

"And you? Did you think so, too?"

"No." Faver met the captain's eyes. "No, I didn't."

Ordoñez looked away. The sun was well up now, and the soldiers were breaking camp. Two men struck the captain's tent and began folding it to be packed. Ordoñez watched them in silence until they carried their bundle away. When he spoke, there was a note of uncertainty in his voice.

"We'll move out soon," he said. "We can go back to La Morita. Or we can ride toward the Río Bravo and the telegraph on the Chihuahua highway."

"You still want to deport me?"

The captain shook his head. He didn't smile. "What will you do now?" he asked.

"Well—I'm trained as a scout. You saw what I did with your men. There must be people who'll pay for that."

People like Zamora, he thought as he said it. Faver saw clearly how it would be, living by his knowledge and his gun, drifting from job to job, town to town, woman to woman. Each job would be less like work and more like murder, each town dirtier and more lawless, each woman less pretty and more mercenary than the last.

"Or there's a section of land in Arizona," he added softly. "I guess I own it."

"If you go back to town, Estella will leave with you."

Faver turned to face him. "And if I don't?" he asked.

Ordoñez smiled. There wasn't much humor in it, but there was some.

"My pride isn't quite as tender as you might think. Especially where Estella is concerned." He stopped smiling and looked at Faver with serious eyes. "It doesn't matter. She will be a good wife."

Fuentes came up diffidently and waited a few paces away until Ordoñez came to speak to him. Faver looked at the troopers, then at the long sweep of the valley, finally toward the ridge where Nantahe lay. The sun was high above the rim and he closed his eyes against the glare.

He'd known, once, that he and Estella were riding different trails. Then, he hadn't seen beyond the end of his own, and the difference didn't seem to matter. Now a new trail stretched ahead. He didn't know where it led, but he would have to follow it alone.

"We're ready to move out," Ordoñez said.

Faver sighed and opened his eyes. "How far to the telegraph?" he asked.

CHAPTER 20

When the Spaniards first came north from the Valley of Mexico, they built a hilltop fortress where the Río Conchos emptied into the Rio Grande. Presidio del Norte became a trading center, a link in the nine-hundred-mile chain of towns along the great Chihuahua Trail. Then war closed the border and trade between San Antonio and Mexico City died, so that Presidio was a forgotten cluster of adobe *jacales* when Jess Faver rode down out of the Sierra del Carmen to cross into the United States.

Faver hardly looked at the town as he guided his pony into the shallows at the ford. His eyes were on a lone figure squatting on the far bank. Randall wore the insignia of a lieutenant colonel now, but he could still wait in the sun with Apache indifference to time and comfort. He rose to his feet as Faver gained the bank.

"I had a telegram," he said by way of greeting. His voice was flat and emotionless. "From the military commander in northern Chihuahua through the War Department, requesting my presence here. I knew it had to be you."

"It was me."

Faver slid from his horse. He'd hoped that, after the passage of time, Randall might greet him as a friend. He should have known better. Randall would no more forget a wrong than would Nantahe, or Faver himself. Blood could only be wiped out with blood.

"I brought you something," he said.

He reached up behind his saddle and yanked the broken Springfield from his blanket roll. He held it for a moment, realizing that this was the end of the hunt, another door closing behind him. Then he tossed it on the sand at Randall's feet.

The officer looked down, taking in the carbine's smashed breechblock and shattered stock. There was a question in his eyes when he raised them to Faver.

"Nantahe? Chicuelo?"

"They're dead," Faver said flatly. "It's over." He waited a moment, then shrugged. "Unless you still want to take me back for trial, that is."

Randall seemed not to hear the last part. "You wouldn't know," he said. "Old Crook got together with General Howard—God knows how, they hate each other's guts—and Welsh of the Indian Bureau. They're working to get the scouts released."

"Through channels?" Faver felt a trace of his old bitterness, but it passed. "I'm glad."

"Yes, through channels, with some political pressure thrown in. And it's working. The scouts will be back in San Carlos within the year."

Faver stooped and checked the pony's cinch strap. He looped the reins over the saddle horn.

"Some of them will," he said. "The ones who haven't died from fever, or from being caged up."

· Randall's face reddened with anger. "Is your way better, Faver? Nantahe, Chicuelo, old Chan-desi—are they better off?"

"I don't know. Maybe. At least, they had a run for it."

"And now they're dead—along with how many others?" Randall pointed to the carbine. "Does that clear your conscience?"

Without answering, Faver swung into the saddle. Randall had arrested the scouts, had taken them to prison. He hadn't liked it any better than Faver had, but he'd seen it as his duty, and it wasn't Faver's right to judge him.

A man dropped a stone into the water. The ripples spread, taking strange forms, going into places he hadn't expected. At last, the ripples died away and the surface of the lake was still.

"You live with your conscience, Colonel. I'll live with mine."

Slowly, the hard lines of Randall's face sagged. There was pain in his eyes when he looked at Faver, pain and a grudging understanding.

"God help us both, then," he said.

Faver lifted a hand to him. Then he kicked the pony's flanks and turned its head west, toward Arizona and home.

DATE DUE